Also by Richard Bach

Stranger to the Ground
Biplane
Nothing by Chance
Jonathan Livingston Seagull
A Gift of Wings
Illusions
There's No Such Place as Far Away
The Bridge Across Forever
One
Running from Safety
Out of My Mind
Rescue Ferrets at Sea
Air Ferrets Aloft

RICHARD BACH

THE FERRET CHRONICLES

Illustrated by the Author

Ferret House Press

Writer Ferrets: Chasing the Muse

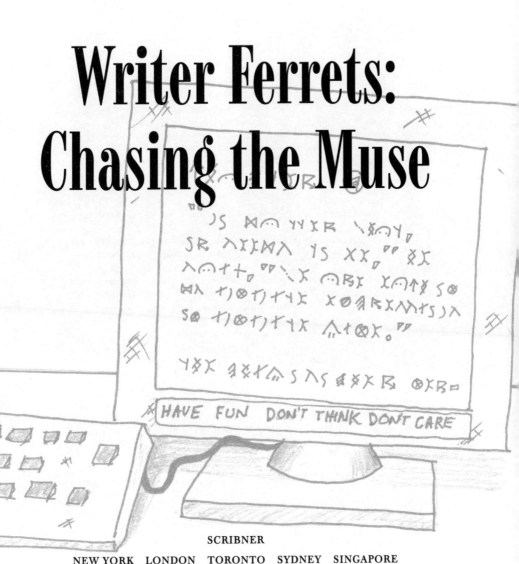

HAVE FUN DON'T THINK DON'T CARE

SCRIBNER

NEW YORK   LONDON   TORONTO   SYDNEY   SINGAPORE

Scribner
1230 Avenue of the Americas
New York, NY 10020

SCRIBNER and design are trademarks of Macmillan Library Reference USA, Inc.,
used under license by Simon & Schuster, the publisher of this work.

For information regarding special discounts for bulk purchases,
please contact Simon & Schuster Special Sales at 1-800-456-6798
or business@simonandschuster.com

Designed by Carla J. Stanley
Text set in Fry's Baskerville

Manufactured in the United States of America

1   3   5   7   9   10   8   6   4   2

Library of Congress Cataloging-in-Publication Data
Bach, Richard.
Writer ferrets: chasing the muse/Richard Bach.
p. cm.
1. Ferrets—Fiction. 2. Authors—Fiction. 3. Authorship—Fiction. I. Title.

PS3552.A255 W75 2002
813'.54—dc21
2002075853

ISBN 0-7432-2754-9

Writer Ferrets: Chasing the Muse

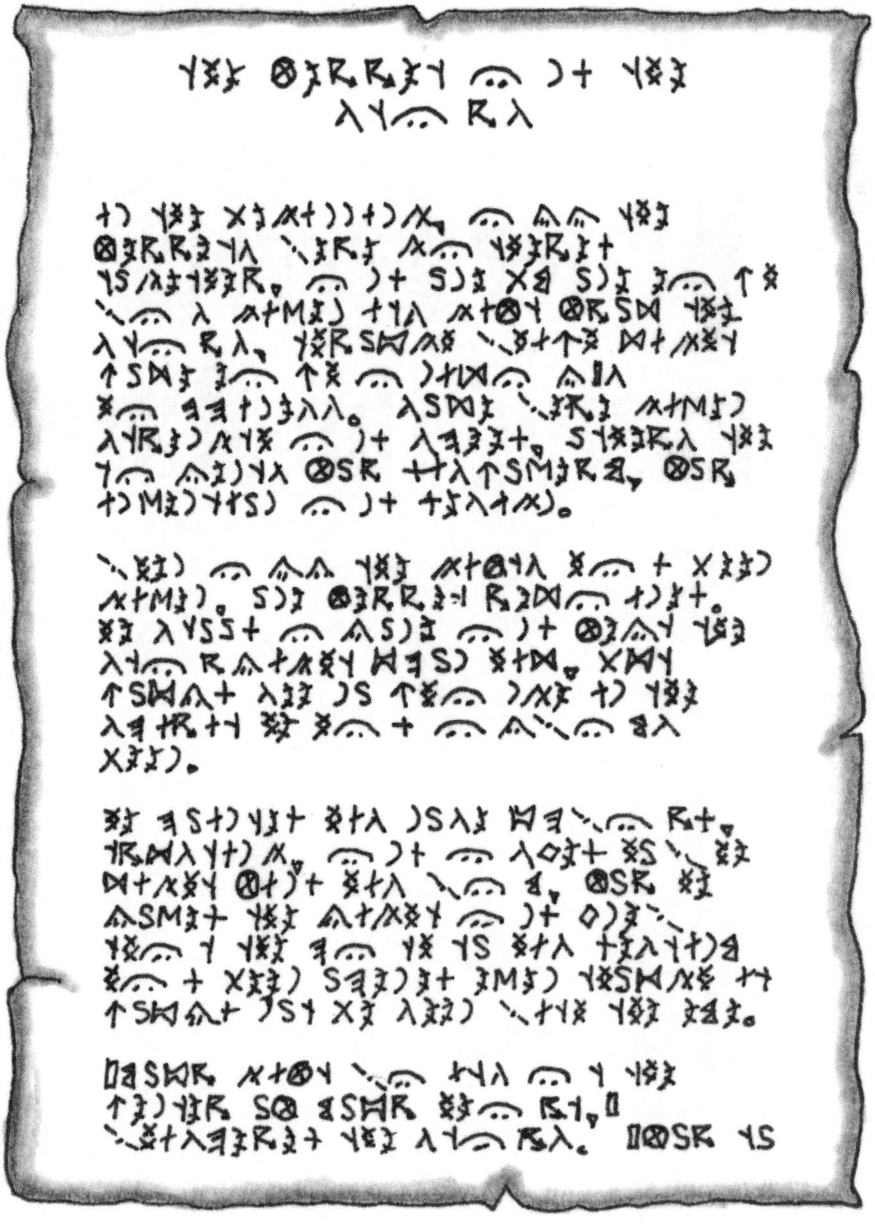

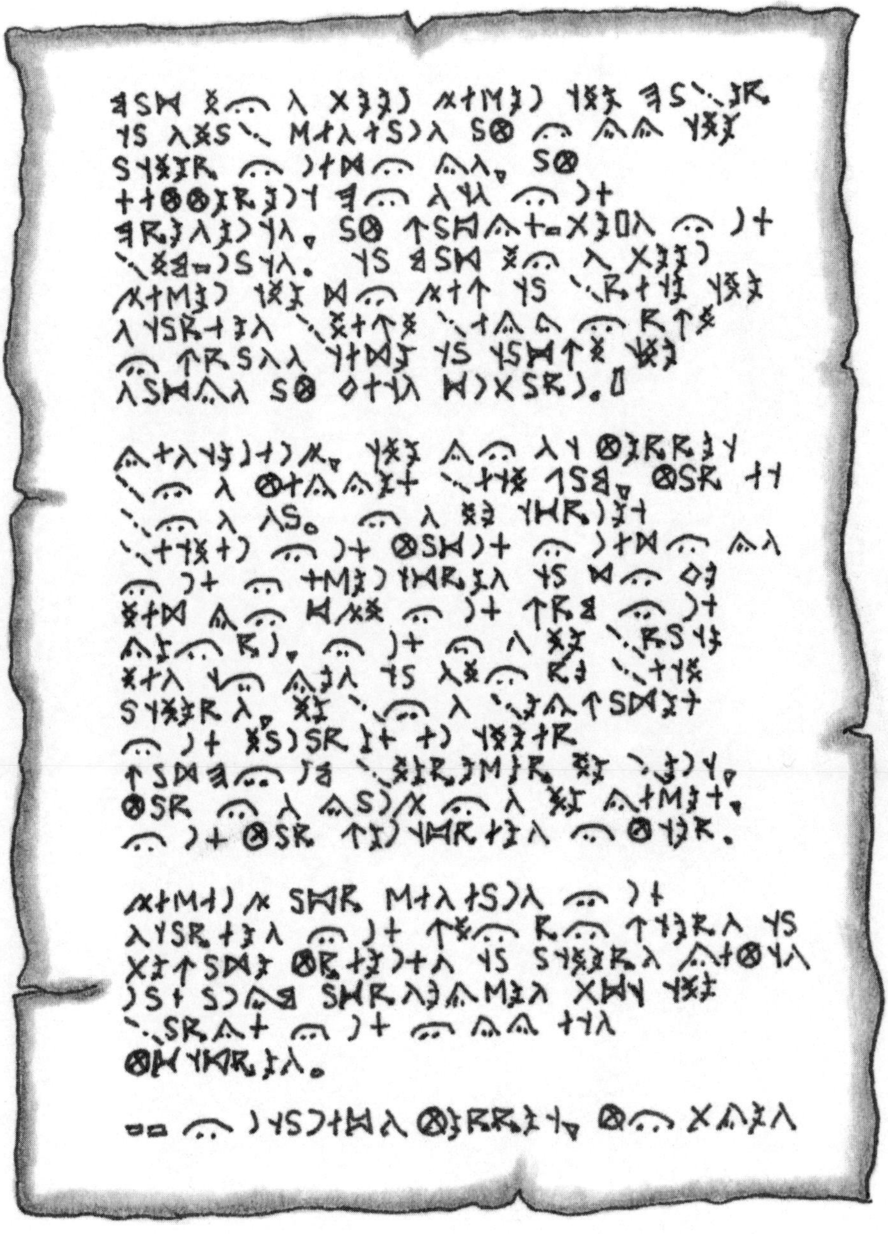

The Ferret and the Stars

In the beginning, all the ferrets were gathered together, and one by one each was given its gift from the stars, through which might come each animal's happiness. Some were given strength and speed, others the talents for discovery, for invention and design.

When all the gifts had been given, one ferret remained. He stood alone and felt the starlight upon him, but could see no change in the spirit he had always been.

He pointed his nose upward, trusting, and asked how he might find his way, for he loved the light and knew that the path to his destiny had been opened even though it could not be seen with the eye.

"Your gift waits at the center of your heart," whispered the stars. "For to you has been given the power to show visions of all the other animals, of different pasts and presents, of could-be's and why-not's. To you has been given the magic to write the stories which will arch across time to touch the souls of kits unborn."

Listening, the last ferret was filled with joy, for it was so. As he turned within and found animals and adventures to make him laugh and cry and learn, and as he wrote his tales to share with others, he was welcomed and honored in their company wherever he went, for as long as he lived, and for centuries after.

Giving our visions and stories and characters to become friends to others lifts not only ourselves but the world and all its futures.

—Antonius Ferret, *Fables*

CHAPTER 1

Budgeron Ferret drew the shades of his tiny attic writing room, unplugged the wall lamp, slipped a white silk scarf around his neck.

What's wrong? he thought in the gloom. Can my trouble be the ceremony itself?

Hollow, tense, he turned to his task, the tips of his ears bending now and then against the low angled ceiling of the room. He lifted the typewriter from the desk, set it on the floor. From the closet he took a wide green blotter, a rosewood case, an ancient oil lamp. He set the case gently at the rear of the desktop, the blotter in front, squaring the edges precisely, placed the lamp alongside.

He was a handsome ferret, the golden fur of his body darkening to ink at the tip of his tail. The mask around his eyes, equally dark, shaped a crisp *W,* a feature that other animals found compelling.

If it's my ceremony that's wrong, he thought, how do I fix it? Does it work because I believe it will work? What happens if I stop believing?

Next the writer struck a match and touched it to the lamp, a flame never lit but for this occasion. He watched the glow lift and settle, the color of an ancient key, peaceful soft reflections in polished silver.

Placing the chair just so in front of the desk, he seated himself. Everything the same, it had to be, as the day he wrote the first sentence.

Sliding open one of two small drawers, he lifted a tiny crystal pot of violet ink and set it in its place on the desk. He removed the cork and put it carefully by the jar, closed the drawer.

From the second drawer he selected a goose-feather quill, its point clean and bright. He laid the quill carefully to the right of the ink and cork.

He nodded, satisfied. Save for the growing terror within him, all was in order.

With the side of his paw he polished the rosewood case, slowly opened the lid. His heart fluttered as he touched his unfinished manuscript.

Where Ferrets Walk
by
Budgeron Ferret

Though he knew it word for word, he read his book yet another time.

Sadly, Count Urbain de Rothskit stood upon his paws by the edge of the castle turret and watched rosy-whiskered dawn push her nose under the tent of night.

The . . .

Here the manuscript ended.

Thus launched into the process of creation, the author sighed. It had a wonderful tension, he thought, yet something wasn't right with the novel that would set the world of ferret literature on its tail.

Did *sadly* mean "without happiness," which the writer intended, or "unfortunately," which he did not?

Was it necessary to write *stood upon his paws?* What else would his hero stand upon?

Did *by the edge of the castle turret* hint that Rothskit was about to jump? His Count was not suicidal.

Rosy-whiskered dawn sounded as fresh as the moment he wrote it, and he liked *the tent of night.* That was good.

He dipped quill-point to ink, lifted it toward the paper. It was time to continue the sentence.

He sighed again, waiting for the adventure that would follow *The . . .*

He wrote *dawn . . .* and stopped. He could not imagine a word to follow that one.

Silence curled in about him, tightening, the coils of a jungle constrictor.

CHAPTER 2

It's THIN AIR, the high country in Montana, and cold. It's hills and plains, sudden low cliffs cut by streams of liquid diamond, through lime-color clouds of summer alder and cottonwood.

Monty Ferret's Rainbow Sheep Resort and Ranchpaw Training Center was a dozen buildings at the center of open wilderness range, pasture and mountains and forest, parched desert and sudden deep lakes, stretching to the horizon in every direction.

"Hup! Hup! *Hya!*"

His first day at the Center, his new red bandana tied stiff and bright about his neck, ranchkit Budgeron Ferret had stood no taller than the middle bar of the corral, eyes wide at what he saw within.

"C'mon! *Go-go-go!*" Inside the corral, a burly ferret on a powerful delphin shouted and whistled, his mount stamped and snorted not ten paws from the pod of sheep.

Each of the woolly creatures a separate pure color, cherry and mint, lemon and plum, instead of stampeding, the Rainbows stood unfrightened, gazed in the direction of the ranchkits, curious to see the new arrivals. One lamb, blue as a twilight sky, yawned.

Monty Ferret, the sheep whisperer, rode to the edge of the corral, looked down upon his ten newest ranchkits.

"So you see," he said, the picture of calm, "shouting and carrying on, that's not goin' to get you anywhere with these animals. They're guests here same as you, except with them we have contracts for the best wool in the world."

He lifted his wide-brimmed ranchpaw hat, brushed back the fur of his brow. "These animals are cloned, they were born in a laboratory, but every Rainbow's an individual. They're beautiful, they're proud, they love the wilderness.

"The one thing they lack," he said, replacing his hat, "is outdoor skills. Their sense of direction isn't as good as yours and mine, they'll get to thinking and wander off, they'll forget to eat, sometimes. That's why you're here. You're going to be their guides, this season."

While he spoke to the young ferrets, the rainbows turned and trotted near, as though they knew what was coming next.

"I suspect you brought some treats from the bunkhouse, kits. You might offer to share some, and watch how these animals behave. . . ."

Budgeron slipped his backpack to the ground, knelt and found the treats, alfalfa hay pressed in soybean oil, the shape and size of broccoli coins. The sheep stretched their noses toward the snacks, took them politely, nibbled them down and stretched for more.

Monty watched, continued his introduction. "Kits, life's not gonna be easy here this summer. Sunup comes early and you'll be runnin' hard till late, no more'n six naps a day."

The kits looked at each other, wordless.

"You've got a lot to learn about ridin', about livin' on the land, findin' your way through the forest and the plains, about always puttin' the Rainbows' comfort before your own. But you'll be ranchpaws by summer's end, and I reckon you'll find it's been worth your trouble."

Swiftly had the kits become friends, Budgeron and Strobe and Boa and Alla and the rest, their hammocks side by side in the bunkhouse, their places together in the dining hall, their delphins in adjoining stalls.

Together they curried their mounts and cleaned stables. They learned to saddle and bridle and ride, to orient themselves by sun and stars, a skill uninteresting to the happy-go-lucky Rainbows, who depended on the ranch-paws to know which way home and how long to get there.

Budgie Ferret had been different, that summer, from the other kits: he wore his crimson bandana and wide-brim ranchpaw hat as they did, he carried bedroll and canteen and many-blade utility knife, but as well he brought note-books and pencils, packed carefully away in his saddlebag.

Spare moments he unwrapped these and wrote pictures of the land around him. He wrote scenes and dialogue, funny stories and scary ones, he wrote what he saw and thought and felt, homesick sometimes, exhilarated others, com-mitting his heart to yellow notepaper.

For all this Western adventuring, he didn't count himself happy unless he had *done* something, unless he had taken some action upon the world around him, and that action was to write what he saw and what he thought.

At the end of the summer, bandana faded nearly to white by sun and rain, Budgeron Ferret had returned to the city self-reliant, independent, confident of his ability to survive in the wilderness and to be a worthy companion and leader to other animals.

On the bus home, he read his dusty, rain-spattered journal, bright colors and songs and scents of high-plains nights and noons, talks remembered word for word, tales of his friends along the trail and around the campfire.

In the pages, summer was alive again.

"I'll be a writer one day," he whispered.

Way down within, his muse listened. It stirred and happily sniffed the air.

CHAPTER 3

 It HAD BEEN two thousand words a day, in the beginning, for more days than Budgie cared to count. Story after story to magazines, Budgeron Ferret received scores of rejection slips, rejection cards, rejection form letters, rejection letters with notes:

"Not quite . . ."

"Try us again . . ."

"Sorry about this one."

Taking these for encouragement, refusing to quit, he had made one sale, another, then sold a pair of adventure tales to the leading magazine for young ferrets.

"You have a particular charm, writing for kits," the editor had written. "You treat our readers as equals, you leave them higher than where you found them.

"Checks enclosed for *Lost on the Prairie* and *Hard Ride to Devil's Fork*. We solicit such additional stories as you feel would be at home in *Kits' Gazette*."

Long-term he would be no kits' writer, he thought, but he liked the compliment, pinned the letter to his office wall.

His first book struck without warning, wrote itself in one bright flash, a kit's journey through the seasons and through a lifetime. *One Paw, Two Paws, Three Paws, Four Paws* sold at once, his first publishing contract.

"*YES!*" he had cried to his empty office. "*Thank you, stars!*"

Within, his muse had smiled.

Surfing a wave of exhilaration, Budgeron Ferret gave his notice at the Black Ermine, found a waiter to replace him, served tables one final day to say good-bye to his friends, turned full-time to his stories.

He had become a writer.

He talked to himself, brave hope through the silence that is a writer's home. "The alphabet is public domain," he said. "Every letter I need is in front of me this minute, on my keyboard now, enough for a thousand books! All I have to do is find the right order for the letters, one after the other. . . ."

Yet, it isn't letters that make a writer, and he knew it. It's ideas that do that, characters come alive, the alphabet a net of light one throws to catch the spinning what-ifs, the pinwheel star systems of the mind, hauling them close for the pleasure of like spirits.

One Paw, Two Paws . . . was published to few reviews and modest sales. Some parents bought the slim volume to read to their kits, others bought it regardless of age, for the kit within.

"The ones who buy your book," his publisher told him, "they love it. But it's been slow catching on."

Neither a bestseller nor a stone disappeared in the pond of literature, his first book sold quietly and steadily without advertisement, one ferret occasionally telling another that it was a happy read.

Mornings found him in the park, then, not rich, not famous, an established young writer. About his neck the knitted scarf from his mother against the autumn breeze, on his lap a pad of yellow notepaper, in his paw a felt-tip pen, in his heart ferrets zany and brave, ferrets unlearned and ferrets wise, all of them characters to tell his stories, characters with stories of their own to tell.

Quality through quantity. He wrote the words and taped them, a thin motto at the top of his writing pad, and that's the way it seemed to be. How his work improved with practice! The more he wrote, the deeper and broader grew his stories, the easier they became to write.

There was something about the air, those mornings in the park, that moved him. It made no difference if he didn't feel inspired, if he didn't feel like writing, if he didn't know what words to put on the paper. He sat at his favorite bench, listened to the birds, then touched pen to pad and he wrote.

The more he wrote, the more there was to write, two thousand words a day, most often more. How much to say from what he had lived and thought, how much to tell about the family of Budgeron look-alikes, scouts and swashbucklers that vaulted and spun through his mind!

Three hours gone in an eye-blink at the park, he'd bring his pad of yellow paper home and type the words he'd written.

"Words on paper!" he told himself. "Words in the air don't matter. If I don't have words on paper I'm not a writer, I'm a talker! No words on paper, how can I improve a sentence? No words on paper, what's to work with, what's to send the publisher, Budgeron?

"So simple. No mystery. *WORDS ON PAPER!*"

He printed the sign in big letters, pinned it to the wall in front of his desk.

Typing finished, a sliver of fruit, a raisin or two, a vitamin cookie. Afternoons he edited his stories, rewriting until he could improve them no more. Then he typed it all again, fresh.

Into the drawer each tale would go at last, to cool for weeks while the next one began. Finally another read, another rewrite, and when he could no longer contain his excitement over the finished work, into its envelope and off it would go to the publisher.

No cover letter to the editor, in those envelopes. No *I hope you'll like the story.*

"Of course I hope you'll like the story," he said to his walls, "or I wouldn't have sent it!"

He kissed his manuscripts good-bye, before he dropped them in the mail, each on its own, no author nearby to help. "Don't be frightened," he whispered at the mailbox. "Speak for yourself!"

To be writing well and yet get rejections, Budgeron Ferret discovered, that is no fun. But a good story returned, he'd shake his head at the house that sent it back, stamp a new envelope and ship it out straightaway to the next, unchanged, until finally one of them had the sense to realize that it beheld the work of Budgeron Ferret, quality writer.

"The day will come," he vowed once, unhappy with the mail, "I am going to build a writing room in my house. I will build that room and I will paper the walls with these very rejection slips, and I will stand in the middle of the room, and I will laugh at you all!"

Just home from the park one Tuesday, answering his telephone, he heard a snarl of lions, menacing, a glad sound from his kithood.

He listened patiently as the snarls faded into the jungle. "Hi, Willow," he said at last.

From the receiver her soft, earthy voice. "Hi, Budge. I need to know how my brother the famous writer is spending his day."

"You know how I'm spending my day," he said. "I'm writing. Let me guess: you've got something on your mind, you can't wait to tell me. Why am I all of a sudden a famous writer?"

"What I was wondering . . ." she said, "have I ever told you about the volunteer at school? She comes once a week and reads to my kits while I run to staff meetings and other things educational?"

CHAPTER 4

H E HAD NOTICED her for several weeks, a slender figure
who came early mornings, Monday through Thursday, to
the same spot by the lakeside, a bag of seeds in her paw for
the sparrows, bread for the ducks. She would spread the
food around her, sit quietly as the creatures came nearby
for their breakfast. Then she would open a book and
read. She always came alone, he noticed, she always
brought food for the park animals, always a book to read.

Other ferrets would come and go, kits on an off-school day
with their little sailboats, with bell-balls to chase on the

grass, grown-up animals with cameras for the park scenes, or sketchpads and pencils.

She was, like himself, a constant.

She'd noticed him, too, he thought, she had to. Same scarf every day, same yellow pad. What she couldn't know was that he sat here Friday mornings, too, and weekends.

They sat not so very far apart, and respecting privacy, never did they say hello.

The days passed, his writing broken and distracted as he watched her stretch her slender paw and offer food to the geese and ducks. They weren't afraid, came close, content when she left that she had given them all she could.

She departed early after her visit one Thursday morning. Budgeron, having lost the thread of his writing, studied trees in the opposite direction.

When he turned back, she was gone, ducks and a single goose pecking the crumbs she had left.

Odd, he thought, that she should leave so suddenly. He looked again. The place was empty but for a book, lying on the grass where she had been. He rose and looked for her down the pathway through the park, but there was no sign of her.

"You left your book," he said quietly. How could she do that? Was she late for work, late for a meeting, that she had rushed away without it?

"Shall I rescue it," he said, "hold it till tomorrow?"

At last his highest sense of right told him to take her book under his protection, return it to her when next she came. He could think of no reason why she would deliberately have left it behind.

He walked to the place, knew before he touched the cover, lifted the book with the strangest sense of destiny.

It was *One Paw, Two Paws,* it was his own book she had left on the grass.

His heart raced. He looked up for her once again, feeling himself an intimate stranger, in spite of his best intentions toward her privacy, entering the life of the young animal with whom he shared the green morning hours.

On his way home, her book in his paw, he realized: tomorrow would be Friday. She would not return to the park until Monday next.

And then, that moment, he knew.

The halls were crowded with kits, and he asked one of them where Willow Ferret's classroom could be found. "That way, sir." The little one stood tall, pointed. "At the end of the hall, it's room 410."

"Thank you," said Budgeron.

"You're welcome! I'm . . ." The kit paused, remembering. "I'm glad to have been of help!" Then, thrilled with the chance to have practiced a courtesy lesson with a stranger, he dropped to his four paws and scampered away.

Ah, the Major Courtesies class, Budgeron remembered, and the advanced Minor Courtesies. *Whatever harm I would do another, I shall first do to myself.*

How many times he had used that principle, how much remorse it had saved! Manners for Ferrets, what a pleasure that class had been, and The Power of Polite. Only when he was grown had he realized how important, how instantly practical it was, the simplest kindness and caring to others—respect for elders, respect for peers, respect for kits.

He found the door and a placard, *Miss Willow Ferret,* looked through the glass. His sister was nowhere to be seen.

The class was beginning, kits settling in a half-circle around a trim grown-up animal. She turned, reaching for a book, glanced up and saw him, watching, the writer in his knitted

Miss Willow Ferret

scarf. A quick wave of her paw, a dazzling smile, then she turned back to the kits.

A flood of warmth swept through him, a wall of heat. It was Danielle Ferret, with whom he had been sharing his green mornings, Danielle and he alone together day by day. Danielle who loved her park and her ducks and her books.

As he watched through the door glass, over her shoulder at the youngsters, the volunteer waited till they were settled and quiet, all noses and whiskers, all the little masks turned toward her. Then she began to read.

"Once upon a time," he heard faintly, through the glass, "by the edge of a great ocean, there was a party of kits, out for a romp. Adventurous they were, but not very wise . . ."

Budgeron watched for a long moment, then he smiled. He turned and walked down the corridor and out of the school. There was no hurry. He would meet her in the park come Monday, he would bring the book, and seeds and bread crumbs, and he would say hello to Danielle Ferret.

CHAPTER 5

IN THE GLOW of the polished old lamp, Budgeron Ferret looked back on those days and yearned for confidence once again.

Why can't I finish the first page? he thought. What follows rosy-whiskered dawn pushing her nose under the tent of night?

There came a gentle knock at the door, and it opened the width of a small paw. "Budgie," called Danielle softly. "Breakfast anytime . . ."

The door eased shut.

The writer sighed. Time passes swiftly on an empty mind, the morning wasted by. He rose from the desk, blew out the lamp, replaced the page in its gleaming box.

He cleaned the quill, set it back in its drawer, put the crystal ink pot, blotter and manuscript away, lifted the typewriter back to the desk.

His literary supernova had not yet lit off, and for the first time he feared that perhaps it never would.

CHAPTER 6

DANIELLE FERRET met him in the little kitchen, a beautiful animal: fur brushed and shining, an oval of snow around her ebon mask, her eyes bright to see him.

He sat at the table, smoothed the mended gingham in front of him with his paw, felt the tiny stitches that healed the torn cloth. How lucky can I get? he thought. She could have had any ferret she wished, for her mate. And she chose me.

"Happy Wednesday," she said, "happy Waffle Day." She placed his favorite breakfast in front of him, crisp orange-butter goodness, a pitcher of warm honey, a glass of milk. "How's the book this morning?"

"It's coming along," he told her.

"Two thousand words today?" She knew his writing pace for kits' stories.

He hadn't mentioned that his classic-literary-novel pace was slower.

"One," he said. All morning, and he had written "dawn." He took a bite of breakfast, in order not to speak.

"Anything you'd want to read to me, Budge? I'd love to hear . . ."

He nodded. "These are wonderful waffles, Danielle. Thank you."

"You're having a little trouble with it, aren't you?" She watched his eyes. "Just a little?"

She stood and walked around the table, leaned down and touched her nose to his, looked at him close up, unblinking, solemn. "You are a great writer, Budgeron Ferret, a great writer, and I won't hear anything different. You will change the world with your words. You will!"

She moved back, nodded *that's that*. Then she took her seat again across the table.

"Danielle . . ." How can she believe in me? he thought. Writing so hard, so long, just a few stories in kits' magazines and one small book to show for it. Drawers of rejection slips, us in this little apartment. Not my apartment, hers. My novel is doomed.

"We have a beautiful future, Budgeron."

"What makes you so *sure*?"

Before she could say, the kitchen clock struck six. She looked up, startled that the time had gone. "Nearly eleven," she said. "I'll be late."

She rose from the table, bent to kiss his nose, lifted her pawdicure bag from its place by the door.

"I just know, sweetheart!" she said. "Write from your highest!"

"It won't be long, Danielle," he told her, filled for a moment with her hope and vision. "Someday you won't have to work."

She flashed him a smile. "I like my work and you know it. Everyone has a story. All day, I make paws bright and listen to stories. All day, every day, chapters in a book, if I write what I hear. We can both be writers!" She waved brightly. "See you tonight, hon."

"Love you," he said.

He smiled, after she left, stirred by his mate's belief. *I can write this book!* I'm born a writer. I read stories when I was a kit, I listened to stories, I wrote stories. *The Polar Bear and the Bad Badger. What Happened to Charlie Chickadee? The Lonely Grasshopper.* Three stories before they trusted me with ink, and those were fine stories, I love them still! *How can I believe I am not a writer?*

Filled with conviction, trusting experience, he rose and climbed the stairs to his writing room, flung himself gladly into his chair. Write from my highest? Write what I know? Write what matters to me? Easy!

Not bothering so much as to square his typewriter to the desk, his paws blurred at once over the keys. He wrote a story that appeared unplanned before him, a flashing of wings, an adventure that filled him with pleasure. Indifferent to all but the scenes within his mind, he stood out of the way of his story and he wrote faster than he had written in a very long time.

CHAPTER 7

"DANIELLE, the littlest kit could have tumbled me with a pounce when Federico told me who she was!"

The pawdicurist stopped at the news to come, her claw-buffer frozen in the air. "She wasn't who you thought, Enriquette?"

"I could have sworn! You'd have done the same. They made a match like royalty, they were so perfect together!"

"'Such a beautiful little thing . . .' Could you believe I said that to poor Federico, reminding him it might be time to settle down: 'Such a beautiful little thing!' I'm seeing white veil, I'm hearing 'We Two Ferrets,' I'm tasting winter snow-water. . . ." Enriquette's voice trailed off.

"And what was wrong with that?" asked Danielle. She set her client's left front paw softly into a bowl of warm oil and fresh lavender petals, crystal marbles at the bottom to touch. She lifted the right front paw, patted it dry, began to buff the claws, not too softly, not too brisk, a moth sound in the quiet. Where is this story going?

"Why, his tail bottlebrushed, he looked at me as if I had just toddled out of the burrow. He took her paw and he said, 'Enriquette, my dear, I'd like you to meet my sister!'"

Danielle caught her breath, shocked.

Her mask the color of ginger, the pawdicurist's elegant client trembled with glee at her own gaffe. "Well, when we touched noses, I couldn't help it, I started laughing. I was going to marry poor Federico to his own sister!"

Her clients at Pretty Paws were her friends. Danielle loved them, she cared that they were happy. Each morning before work, the salon's youngest pawdicurist stopped at the flower stalls for fragrant petals, and as she came to know the flower ferrets, listening to their happy gossip, she found who was ordering flowers for whom.

She made her own exfoliating scrubs for the paws, candle-warmed paraffin and essential-oil treatments, mixed a rainbow of pastels into moisturizing creams of cocoa butter and fresh flowers, scented lotions and wraps, carefully she selected paw files and pumice stones. Bright old ferret jigs and reels played in her cubicle. At the end of the session she gave each client a last few minutes of paw reflexology and sent them on their way.

Danielle Ferret collected true-life stories. The more bizarre and startling, the more they clung to her mind, exotic gems treasured and carefully stored.

Though she hadn't dared to set the stories down in notes, for the minutes between clients she moved herself into their lives, relived their adventures with a smile and sometimes a tear for the choices they had made.

On her walk home of an evening not long after, dodging traffic, one animal in a sea of others, she considered writing for the hundredth time since those careless words to Budgeron: we can both be writers. All these stories within . . .

Now she knew it could be so, if she wanted. Of course she would never be a writer of Budgeron's stature. The only way he could stall his success would be for him to stop writing, and that would never happen. Her mate would change ferret culture, lift it higher than ever it had been.

Yet there's no reason why I couldn't write, too, she thought, some little tales, the kind I love to hear. What fun that would be!

Charmed with the idea, she failed to notice the taxicab drifting high speed around the corner, rushing uptown.

Budgeron has his future, she was thinking as she stepped into the street, and I have mine as well. It would be fun, both of us writing. I could learn . . .

Denison "Lion" Ferret did not question why the trim animal ahead had lost her mind. He did not think, but spun the wheel hard right, stabbed the brakes beyond the edge of rolling friction, a screech that trembled window glass three stories high, blue smoke exploding from all tires.

Ferrets left and right heard and saw, flew to rescue, instant reflexes too late to save her.

Instead of sliding broadside into Danielle, Lion's cab lurched sideways to a stop a tenth-second from her body, close enough that the driver could reach from his window and touch her paw.

Which he did. He looked up into eyes wide with fright, the pedestrian clutching her pawdicure bag for security.

A sigh of relief from the cabdriver. "I guess it's not your time, miss."

At once they were surrounded by others, Lion's cab and the crowd of help still wreathed in a cloud of burnt rubber. The traffic light changed, the would-be rescuers found all parties alive and well, the smoke drifted away.

Danielle gasped once, and then again. She covered his paw with her own. "I'm so sorry . . . what a foolish thing! I was thinking . . . I didn't look . . ." She turned to the crowd. "He saved my life!"

Her paw trembled on Lion's, he steadied her a second longer. "It's all right now, miss," he said. "It's over."

She nodded, starting to breathe again. "Thank you!"

He removed his paw from hers. "Mighty powerful dreams, walking like that into traffic. You take care now and make those dreams come true!"

The driver touched the brim of his cap to her and his machine moved away.

Trembling still as the crowd reminded her to be careful and went its way back to the sidewalks, Danielle wondered. Had the driver been an angel ferret, handing her a new life, a new life writing? Not the Great Ferret Novel, but something— stories of ordinary animals, the kind she loved to hear.

She looked both ways at the next corner, crossed when the light changed to WALK.

I mustn't write what I've been told, she thought, but what harm in fitting parts here, parts there, no one could recognize? A collection of stories, just for fun.

A moment later, she slowed and stopped on the sidewalk, others hurrying past, left and right. Not a collection. A novel! A *romance* novel!

There's no reason in the world why I can't, she thought. For the fun of it, of course, just for fun. It may never be good enough to publish, but what a pleasure, the pages accumulating, the book taking shape, even if I'd be its only reader.

She ran up the steps to the apartment, slowed at the door.

For the fun of it.

She was too shy to share her plan with her husband. He was the writer, published time and again, she the novice, untalented, a kit at a grown-up's game.

She'd tell him later.

She turned the knob and entered.

"I'm home!"

A call from above, the sound of paws on the stairs. "Danielle! Welcome home!" A different Budgeron from the morning, her husband met her with a glad hug. "How was your day?"

She remembered her clients and their stories, and her decision. "Wonderful! How was yours?"

"Do you know what? Guess what."

"The book is finished," she said, kidding.

He nodded, as happy as she had ever seen him.

"I can't believe it, Budgie! It's finished? *Where Ferrets Walk* is finished? Congratulations, dearest wonderful best writer in the whole world!"

"*Where Ferrets Walk*?" he said. "Oh. No. That's not finished. I wrote a different book. What's finished is *Bevo the Hummingbird*!"

"*Bevo . . .*"

He nodded. "Remember, I told you? When I was a kit. My mom made stuffed animals for me. Bevo was the first, he slept on my pillow. And the story came—*whoof!*—it was already there. All I had to do was type."

"Why, of course! Bevo the Hummingbird! Do you love it?"

She could tell, the look in his eyes.

She touched his paw. "Read it to me?"

"Maybe you'd like to read it yourself. I need to know where the story slows for you, where you lose interest, where it's—"

"Read it to me," she said. "Please, Budgeron. I need to hear it. Your voice."

Her mate knew better than to argue. She had her reasons, always she had her reasons. Later she could read the story to herself.

He brought the manuscript to the kitchen table, a plump sheaf of pages neatly typed.

What happened, Budge? she wanted to ask. Why all of a sudden can you fly through this story, write it in a flash, when week after week your literary novel slows you to stone?

But she said not a word. She sat at the kitchen table while he settled in his chair, she watched and listened.

"*It was midnight when Bevo woke,*" he began. "*All about him, the sky was dark. The trees were dark. The moon was dark, and the stars.*"

For an hour he read, until:

"*Happy at last with the creature he had chosen to be, Bevo the Hummingbird tucked his bill under his wing and fell fast asleep.*"

He looked to his mate. "*The End,*" he added.

Danielle opened her eyes, saw her husband through a curtain of tears.

"Budgeron," she said softly. "Oh, Budge. It's beautiful!"

"The raccoons," he asked. "Are they a little too . . . uncivilized?"

"Too nothing!" she cried. "I love the raccoons! It's the most beautiful warm touching story I've ever heard in my life!"

"Maybe when you read it—"

"*Budgie! Listen!* What have you wanted to do since you were a kit? Don't you know? Like *One Paw, Two Paws*! You've done it again!"

Tears glistened still in the writer's eyes from the touching moments of his own story. He trusted her judgment. He had always told his mate that she had a grand story sense, and now she was telling him that his little tale had promise. He agreed. To have touched him so, he knew it did.

He quivered with what had happened that day, his writing a whirlwind that left him breathing fast. He had not invented the story. It had been there all along, unwritten: beginning, middle, end. Every scene, every incident necessary, every one of them had to be, inevitable.

The hummingbird had picked up his self-consciousness and his fears and dashed them aside, uncaring. Bevo had used the ferret's paws, used his thoughts and experience and vocabulary to tell a story that had to be told. Now it was finished, the author churned in its wake, left to glue himself back together as best he could.

Was it publishable? He was still too close to the tale to judge, but he didn't need to struggle for some verdict. It felt perfect, somehow, the story made him happier than any he had written.

Tomorrow he would ask how he had done it, and find no answer. For now, all that mattered was that Bevo the Hummingbird, with all that he dreamed and all that he stood for, had somehow been touched with magic and come to life.

Hurray! the writer thought. A few days smoothing, a little polish, off it goes to the publisher. What good practice! Now to do the same with my novel!

Within, a sigh, crestfallen. Whisper of an unseen voice: Am I a failure as a muse?

CHAPTER 8

DANIELLE FERRET had promised that she would write for the fun of it.

She expected that with time and practice, the words would come quiet and orderly. She expected that whatever character she might invent would be flat and wooden for a long while. She expected to look at a blank page one and begin a long search for her first word.

What Danielle didn't expect was that her first page would explode with the likes of Veronique Sibhoan Ferret, a willful animal caught time and again in webs of her own spinning, in schemes so complicated that her author could barely imagine how they had started or what would happen next.

As Danielle watched the page wide-eyed, as she sometimes stopped and raised a paw to cover her open mouth, Veronique played with the hearts of others the way a kit plays with bell-balls—the more of them tumbling at once, the better the little flirt liked the game.

They're toys, she thought of the strong and gentle males around her. Of what use are toys except for play?

One moment innocent, the next mad for power, the night-masked Veronique laughed to shock her own author as much as to electrify readers of *Miss Mischief.*

By the seventy-fourth page, Veronique was openly plotting to deceive her roommate's long-lost Swedish half brother, Telegaard, fallen hopelessly in love with the vixen.

"You shall never know my name," Danielle's heroine cried to him. *"But if you must, call me . . . Valka!"*

How the vamp had discovered the name of Telegaard's secret first love, the author would not know for many pages. But discover it she had, and Veronique took the name shamelessly, as a leopard, remorseless, devours a different hunter's kill.

All that the pawdicurist once heard within the walls of her cubicle, innocent misunderstandings and exaggerated stories told in the ferret way, to make fun of the teller herself, they tilted and shifted, came spinning out in harlequin suits and sinister intrigues as the author wrote, watching her pages dumbfounded.

From the time they are kits, ferrets are patiently instructed always to live to their highest sense of right. They are showered with love, treated with respect by their parents and by every other animal of their culture. No matter the path they choose for themselves, they run it with grace and honesty and pride.

In a land without envy or malice, without evil or crime or war, in a world of esteem for self and others, the least of ferrets knows that it is equal to the greatest, and they treat each other so.

Never had it been wondered, what if something went wrong, somehow, what if there could be such a thing as a *naughty ferret*? What would she say, how would she act?

Now and here, in the ink from her own pen, Danielle watched Veronique Sibhoan slink forth, she who lived for the moment, self-centered, thoughtless of consequences, uncaring of the highest right.

How shall I shatter that romance? She dangled her toes in the warm ripple-pond, watching the light shimmer in her

own dark fur. How shall I split Carlos and Rikka? After I've finished with Telegaard, I want to play with her raven-whiskered captain for a while. . . .

With a horrified flash of her paw, Danielle swept her manuscript from the kitchen table, a blizzard of snowsheets to the floor.

How can it be, she thought, my husband at the top of the stairs working to bring the Great Ferret Novel into the world, and me below, helping this wicked creature to life!

She gathered the papers left and right, crumpled them, willed her saucy temptress never to draw another breath. Into the fireplace they went, Danielle striking the match. May Budgeron never know what I have done. . . .

Her paw shook, though, the match burned alone for a moment, suspended in air.

Veronique's barely more than a kit, the author thought, she's just pretending to be a naughty ferret. Swept away in a hurricane as a kit, raised by squirrels, untrained in courtesy or friendship or the power of kindness to others, she means no harm. Her challenge is that she must learn grace and understanding from life itself, on her own.

The flame waited.

What kind of creature am I, who would destroy one whose only crime is that she hasn't found her way to love? And how do I know that those she seeks to bring down may not be noble enough to lift her up, instead?

The match burned lower, and finally Danielle let it fall, a lingering trail of smoke.

Budgeron creates literature, she thought. I write a dalliance for grown-ups, a book for the moment. Both are important. Both are fun.

The author lifted the pages, smoothed them against the floor, sat there and read her last lines again. A naughty ferret, indeed. Still, by the end of the story Veronique will have lived the consequences of all that she has done, and how she will have grown!

Danielle settled herself once again at the kitchen table, raised her pen, let the story continue.

"Veronique," asked the captain, stepping from the old entrance tunnel into the light, "have you seen my bowl of raisins?" Her host blinked in the sunshine. "They were here a minute ago."

"Raisins, Carlos?" She swallowed the last one, the bowl fallen silently to the grass beneath the picnic table. "No, I don't see them," she said. "They're not here now. . . ."

CHAPTER 9

W<small>HEN</small> B<small>UDGERON</small> F<small>ERRET</small> came down the stairs next Waffle Day, Danielle knew he was in trouble.

She flashed her glorious smile, hugged him with one paw, the other holding a plate of golden crispness.

His nose twitched in the warm aroma.

The two ferrets sat at their little table. Danielle offered an amber pitcher. "Honey, sweet?"

A wan smile from her mate.

She watched his face. "A thousand words today?"

"There's something I need to tell you, Danielle."

She waited.

His eyes downcast, he took a breath. "The novel is not going well. It is worse than not going well. I wrote a hundred words today and they are all wrong."

He lifted his head, looked at her in anguish. "I tried, Danielle! I flew into that story same as I did with Bevo, but instead of the Count writing himself, instead of the story blasting through me like some wild-away freight train, it . . . I'm pushing on a stone wall. No. I'm pushing on a sponge, a wet sponge. No crash, no fire. Nothing."

He lifted his eyes to the ceiling, waffle untouched. "*Where Ferrets Walk* is a wonderful title, Danielle, a literary genius of a title. All it needs is some . . . and I am *home free,* I am no kits' writer, I'll be an *author!*" He took a breath. "I'll be a real author, at last."

He sighed. "Nothing. I don't have a whisper, what happens to Count Urbain de Rothskit. I like his name, but you know, I really don't like the animal himself. He comes from some different world, he looks down his whiskers at me: I'm not worthy to write his story. He shuts me off!"

oke as if he were warning the Count himself: "If I
get that ferret moving before long, if I have to wait
ith my quill and beg for words, I swear, Danielle,
ng strange is going to happen to him!"

ed. How can my book be such adventure for me,
ht, and his such pain for dear Budgeron, his big
ore the answer could unfold its own reasons,
imed thirteen.

o run," said her husband, his voice lifeless.

e today."

self to the edge of confidence. "Nonsense.
ning. By the time you get home, I'll have a
shed and the Count's going to be brushed
"

"I've never seen you so down, Budge.
r I stay? l can bring you some orange
later on. I think I'd rather stay."

a lot that you'd offer, and I'd ask you
ly bad. Honest. I would. But I am a
m not the pawn of my characters.
t door, I'm going to have a little
le Count. . . ."

nove.

"I will be kind but firm with him, Danielle. Really. Off you go to work. If we don't have groceries, if there'll be no waffles next Wednesday, *that* will be disaster!"

His wife laughed, then rose and kissed him. "That's my Budgie," she said. "Never quit!"

She took her bag from the hook on the door. "See you tonight," she said. "And don't you be too hard on the Count."

CHAPTER 10

T HE TOP of the page was embossed, gold on white, *Books for Kits: A Division of Ferret House Press.*

"Dear Budgeron Ferret," the letter began.

"It is with considerable pleasure that we at Ferret House Press must tell you that we find your story *Bevo the Hummingbird* a delight. Rarely do we encounter such charm and grace in a book for young ferrets, or a theme so uplifting.

"Enclosed is a proposed contract for publication. Because of the demonstrated success of *One Paw, Two Paws . . .*, we would be particularly pleased to become the publisher of this story. We have taken the liberty of increasing the advance payment over our standard terms, and raising the royalty percentage.

"We hope that you will consider ours to be the winning bid for world rights to your story. If you would care to send it to other publishers, however, please feel free to do so, and allow us the opportunity to top whatever terms they might offer.

"With thanks for the kindness of your consideration, we remain, your obedient servants . . ."

Danielle had taken the letter from her husband's frozen paw a moment after he had stumbled down from the office and appeared, wordless, in the kitchen.

She read it once again, aloud. She glanced through the contract attached, saw that the advance payment was an amount many times larger than their life savings.

"Budgie, I think . . . ," she said, dazed. "I think . . ."

She gave the letter back. The pressure of the paper against his numbed paw was enough to topple her husband's body slowly backward to the floor. Danielle, for her part, collapsed more or less straight down.

The clock chimed sixteen, and after that it was quiet in the kitchen.

CHAPTER 11

Five KILOPAWS west of Side-Hop, Colorado, the house rambled over the high range: east of the mountains, south of the river. Soft hills, rising and falling, the colors of a sparkling shallow sea, shimmering like a broad summer moat around them.

Who would have thought, they asked each other, that solitude could become priceless?

With the publisher's advance and high hopes for the success of *Bevo the Hummingbird,* the two ferrets had given up their apartment and moved to the land of Budgie's kithood summer.

Here amid the splendor towering above, whispering below, the author planned to start a new life with Danielle, and to finish his epic novel at last. Surely in this haven from stress he could now find and master his reluctant muse.

From the porch on a fine day they could see their gate, away in the valley. In the months since they had moved, they had heard no sound of traffic or horn, they had seen no other animal save for their friend and ranchpaw Slim, out mornings riding fence.

With the two ferrets lived the hush of wind in the cotton-woods, the whisper of sunlight by day and moonlight in the dark. Peace rustled down on them like a fluffy deep comforter.

In that precious calm the two of them talked and walked. Her husband taught her to care for their delphins Dusty and Lucky, to bridle and mount and take them on long rides. Danielle came to love those times, and she and Budgeron could be found together nearly every morning in the saddle, deep in the quiet of the land.

For all their change and comfort, however, never did they forget what parents and culture had taught: the more gifts we're given, the more we can pass along to other creatures.

His book now a bestseller on the kits'-book list, Budgeron Ferret spent five nights a week in a drawing room he had furnished especially for work on his epic novel. Quill and lamp no longer in the closet, they stood full-time on his desk.

What a gift it would be, *Where Ferrets Walk,* if he could somehow finish the story.

Yet no muse appeared. In fact, he found in time that not only did he lack a muse for this most important work of his life, but he had somehow attracted a wicked antimuse, whose every whisper told him how worthless he was, how bad his writing, how hopeless to wish that his work would grace the libraries or even the nightstands of the literati, of the studied sophisticates in the city he had just departed.

In his office gleamed a new computer, and here he kept the mundane: business correspondence, interviews, a copy of the Bevo story, letters to family and friends.

From this computer Budgie declined his publisher's request for a second Bevo book with a short note: "While I am delighted that my hummingbird has become a success for us all," he wrote, "I am at work on a major historical novel, which I shall submit for your interest when it is finished."

He wandered off, then, to the kitchen, laid out a platter of celery and peanut butter, ringed it in a circle of grapes. He ambled to the porch, where Danielle sat in front of what until lately had been her husband's typewriter.

"Hi, dear," she said absently as he slid into the chair alongside.

The keys rose and fell under her paws, an even, steady click of steels against ribbon and paper. He watched her eyes, knew what she was seeing. She was not looking at the paper in the machine or at the words, but through them, into a different world from this one. Scenes moved, changing moment to moment, close-ups and long shots, actors turning on the set, she reporting the drama as it played in front of her.

He sat near for a long while. How different it is, he thought, writing for fun! He watched the tiny smiles that came and went on her face as the story surprised her, caught her off-balance.

At that moment, Danielle was watching bad Veronique accept, with a flutter of her lashes, an engagement necklace from a ferret whom she had not the least intention of marrying.

"Gunnar, you are kind! Much too kind for the likes of this poor mustelid!"

He slipped the diamonds about her lovely sable fur, sparkles upon sheen.

Veronique turned and gave him a radiant smile. "Do you like them, dearest?"

Without waiting for him to respond, and for a lark, she dashed the poor animal with ice water.

Danielle caught her breath, then laughed, typing steadily.

Budgeron rose without a sound, leaving the plate of snacks on the side table for his mate.

She turned her face toward him, yet her eyes held on the scene within the white paper. "I love you, Budgie," she said, from another universe.

CHAPTER 12

S HE CAME to him in the kitchen, a coral-color paper in her paw as he installed a shelf above the window. She extended it to him without a word, so that he put down his bracket and hammer.

"Why, that looks familiar," he said, but did not take the paper from her. "Let me guess . . ."

He watched her eyes, sad glow of a tear in each, gathered her to him in a gentle embrace.

As she clung close against his chest, as her tears fell, he quoted from memory.

"'Dear Writer: Thank you for your submission. Unfortunately, your manuscript does not meet our publishing needs at this time. Sincerely, The Editors,'" he said. "Is that what it says on the slip?"

She nodded. "Then at the bottom," she sniffed, "somebody wrote, 'Nice try. Too controversial.'" She was trembling.

He held her away for a moment, to see her face. "You got a 'Nice try' on your first submission? Danielle, that's wonderful!" He enfolded her again. "Why, my stories, they sent five of them back, printed slips, before I got my first 'Nice try'!"

"They rejected *Miss Mischief. . . .*"

He felt the trembling. She had failed. It had started as a game, writing for fun. Yet she had done her best, she had laughed with Veronique and she had cried and she had held her breath for that animal, day after day, months till her book was finished, till it was fiction no longer. She loved her heroine and the patient friends who had shown her the way.

Now they're dead, she thought. Veronique, Telegaard, Lisette, wise Balfour. All of them. Rejected.

Budgeron stroked the fur of her neck. "Yes. They've rejected your book. They didn't want it, they sent it back."

He moved half a step, to look in her eyes. "One of the editors liked it, though. She was outvoted, but she liked it enough to tell you her truth and to write that note."

Danielle sighed, released herself from his embrace, brushed her tears, took control of her feelings. "Oh, well. I wrote it for fun, anyway. It felt so good, to finish that manuscript, and write, 'The End'!"

"The two most beautiful words in the language," he said. He did not return to his work. "What are you going to do?"

"I'm sure somebody needs a pawdicurist in town."

"There are worse jobs," he said. He reached for the shelf bracket. "Do you love your book, Danielle?"

"You know I do, Budgie. I wouldn't change a page! Veronique tries to be bad, but she doesn't know how. She's got a wonderful heart, and in the end, the very ferrets she's been mean to are the ones who save her." Tears fell once again. "Oh, Budgeron, I love them! I love my book!"

Calm and strong, her mate stood close, held her again. "If you love your book, what are you going to do with it?"

She stiffened. "I'm not going to throw it away," she cried, *"I will not!"*

"No."

"Why are you looking at me? What am I supposed to do with my book now?" She was close to tears again. *"It's been rejected!"*

"Who rejected it?"

"Does it matter? Bottlebrush Press. They sent it back!"

"Besides Bottlebrush, how many publishers are there in Manhattan?"

"Many," she sniffed. "But if Bottlebrush didn't like it . . ."

"No one else will? Have you ever heard of a book rejected at one house, rejected at ten or twenty, then gets published the twenty-first time and comes out a bestseller?"

He looked at her severely, professor to a kit. "Danielle, it's not whether a publisher likes your book that matters, it's whether *you* like it! When you believe in your story, you're not looking for a whole company to publish it, you're looking for one editor, one animal from your true family, the same taste as yours, same loves, same excitements, and that ferret happens to work at a publishing house, determined to fight if she must to see your book in print!"

Danielle brightened. "And this ferret, you're saying, may be at some other house, not Bottlebrush?"

He nodded.

"So you're saying I ought to try again?"

He did not respond.

"And all it's going to cost me is a return envelope, and the postage?"

He nodded.

"And someday someone's going to accept my book?"

"If they don't, you have another rejection slip for your collection."

A wan smile. "How can I lose?"

The little animal hugged her mate, bounced off to find the address of another publisher.

The kitchen shelves were installed by sunset.

CHAPTER 13

BUDGERON FERRET woke into darkness, breathing hard. The dream that had struck him once had struck again.

A host of animals was calling to him, bears and birds, snakes and wolves and giraffes, voices across a bright lake. No words but his own name, begging his notice.

"Budgeron . . ."

"Budgie . . ."

"B-ron!"

"Budgidear . . ."

"Boucheron-Bvuhlova . . ."

All the voices at once, each calling softly.

He was stepping toward the lake when he heard the sound of hooves on turf. The next moment a giant delphin swept down from the hills, the animal and ferret rider in ancient colors. They looked neither left nor right, the dark figure in the saddle urging his mount to greater speed.

The two struck the water a violent blur, sheets of spray flying.

They galloped through, wild thunders, and were gone, echoes of hooves fading into silence. When the water curtains fell behind them, the voices across the lake were silent.

Empty grass.

No one called his name.

Budgeron Ferret lay in the dark, trembling.

CHAPTER 14

T HAT WAS a hard summer for Danielle Ferret and her manuscript.

The former pawdicurist received another rejection, from a different house, this time "Not quite!" written by paw over the printed text.

Three weeks later, the next, from Sleekwhisker Books:

"Dear Danielle Ferret:

"To say that we were startled upon reading your novel, *Miss Mischief,* would be an understatement. It has caused quite a stir in the office, and, I must admit, some controversy.

"Our sense of right, of course, suggests that we decline your submission as the actions of your heroine are not in the highest traditions of ferret literature and culture.

"Thank you for sending your story. Your writing has fine pacing and adventure. We wish you great success in your future writing and hope you will allow us to consider your next manuscript.

"JoBeth A. Ferret, Associate Editor"

Weeks after her sixth submission, this time to Ferret House Press, she frowned at the mail. Ferret House did not return her manuscript, but sent a rejection envelope anyway.

My husband writes a bestseller for your company, she blazed, you could at least send back my manuscript! Then, shocked at her outburst, she apologized to the stars and realized that she had made no agreement with the company to return her manuscript, and it was in no way bound to do so.

Not eager to see how Ferret House had phrased the rejection, she put the envelope aside.

It wasn't until evening that she opened the mail: bills, an interview request for Budgeron from *Kits Adventure,* the letter from Ferret House.

She sighed. She would paper the walls . . .

"Dear Danielle Ferret:

"Of course you know that your novel, *Miss Mischief,* is a story of behavior that every ferret would consider unacceptable.

"On the other paw, we find your story to be irresistible entertainment. While we certainly do not approve of Veronique Sibhoan's motives or choices, we cannot but admire her determination and infectious insouciance.

"In addition, the power of the manuscript's final chapter, to us, justifies all that has led to it. Veronique is indeed a kit from difficult beginnings, with much to learn about loving, and she learns it with the grandest bravura, at the last possible second.

"Usually we have a clear sense of the sales potential of the books we publish. With your story, we do not. Whether book-loving ferrets will embrace *Miss Mischief* or revile her, we cannot say.

"However, we believe that Veronique speaks for herself, and that holding her whiskers high, unashamed, she will dare her readers to be her judge.

"The offer attached is a modest one, because of the risk in publishing a novel without precedent. You will notice, however, that should the book sell a large number of copies, your profit participation will increase.

"With thanks for the kindness of your consideration that Ferret House Press might be your publisher, we remain, your obedient servants,

"Vauxhall Ferret, President"

Budgie looked up from his desk into a dark satin mask radiant with triumph. He took the letter from her paw, read it, let it drop to the floor. Without rising, he swept his mate into his arms, the two nearly crashing to the floor from the overloaded office chair. He felt sobs of relief against his shoulder, soaking him in happy tears.

"Danielle." His words muffled against her fur. "You did it. Congratulations. You worked hard, day after day, and you did it!"

"Oh, Budgie," she sobbed, "you know it wasn't work. I watched Veronique and I wrote what she did. That little vixen . . ."

After a time he set her on her paws, then stood and went to the kitchen, returned with the bottle of winter snow-water, saved just above freezing for a moment like this.

Danielle was wreathed in delight. "I didn't change a word, Budgeron! I put the same manuscript in a different envelope and I sent it out another time!"

"Why didn't you try Ferret House first thing? They're my publisher!"

"That's why," she said. "Ferret House is *your* publisher. I didn't want . . ." She smiled. "Until I got desperate, I didn't want them to think I was asking for favors."

He touched her nose. "Silly kit! Do you think a publisher is going to spend a fortune publishing your book, some favor to you? How many favors before they're out of business? They're publishing your book because they love your story as much as you do!" He grinned at her. "And because they intend to earn a lot of money from *Miss Mischief.*"

The two animals talked long into the night about what Danielle's future might bring, and sunrise found them in front of the fireplace, nestled in each other's fur, asleep.

CHAPTER 15

BUDGERON READ what he had finished that morning:

" . . . only from that vantage will I be able to study the moon and planets as I need, test my theory of our origins. Yes, I believe it will be necessary to move this entire castle, stone by stone, to the top of the mountain."

"My dear Count!" said the burgomeister. "What will say the Duke de Mustille? Will not your castle on yon hill fall squarely in view from his own?"

"We have spoken about this. He finds my home a pleasure to his eye, and does not object."

"But—"

"Further, I shall pay handsomely every animal that lifts a paw to help me. It is a grand work, that upon which I am embarked. . . ."

"Wrong. Wrong! *Wrong!*" The writer dashed his quill to the blotter, violet ink spraying the soft green.

My kits' stories are life, action and colors everywhere, he thought. My novel, it's stilted, it's false, it's *dull,* turns me to wood. *And I'm the author!* Oh! my poor reader . . .

The truth swept over him, a mantle of stone and lead: *I've forgotten how to write.*

In the long silence that followed, his eyes closed, his nose sank low. It felt like dying, the light ebbing from his mind. This time, though, with the darkness came a voice within, a dragon from the night of his soul.

Who do you think you are, Budgie Ferret? What kind of a fraud, you dare call yourself a writer? Do you so love pain that you torture yourself this way?

He did not respond.

Who cares about you? Your book is no book, and you know it. The pages are sand, worthless. The novel was worthless from the start, it is worthless still, it will be worthless when you finally give up and tear it to shreds.

What a fool you are! To believe that any animal will ever read a word you write about Urbain de Rothskit, or care. A fool, Budgie. You make everything just so, you light your Lamp of Wisdom, and you ply your fancy quill. Go on, Great Writer, try it now! Try hard. What's the next sentence? And why bother? The blank page, it had some value as paper. You wrote on it. Now it's trash.

After a long moment, slowly, the once proud, once confident Budgeron Ferret tilted forward in anguish, until his nose and whiskers rested on the soft blotter.

The ink dried, slowly, on the fallen quill.

The dragon did not disappear.

Your thoughts are logs, jammed in a river, not connected, crazy angles. Your ideas are rocks. Not even. Your ideas are common pebbles, they mean nothing, they're worth less.

Worth less.

Great minds wrote the classics, ages past, and now along comes Budgeron Ferret thinking he's going to write a literary novel that will change the world? Is that likely?

The animal on the desk moved slowly, and only enough that its head rested no longer upon its nose, but upon the side of its face. Its eyes closed.

I'm asking. Is it likely that any novel you can imagine will ever change the world, which was getting along fine before ever you were born and is managing to get along fine without you this very minute?

Silence.

What are the odds that might happen? One in a million? One in how many millions? Are you different from any other creature who ever lived . . . are you so different, let alone better, that any word you write for the halls of literature deserves to be read?

Silence.

Surely there is a better way to spend your time than Where Ferrets Walk. *What a foolish title! What a foolish animal you are!*

Then, in a giant echoing whisper, the dragon recited the names of the great ferret writers through the ages. It was no celebration, but a dirge to hopelessness.

. . . Barthenai . . . Emander . . . Avedoi Merek . . . Chiao Jung-wei . . . Miguelita Ferez . . .

soul in your writing. Not soul. No. What am I trying to say? There's something in everything you do . . . it's in *One Paw, Two Paws . . .* , it's in *Bevo.* I care about Bevo because he's got my heart in his wings. He's Bevo, but he's *me,* too! I don't know how you do that. I can't write that way. Veronique's not me. She's not any ferret I've ever known. She's fiction, but Bevo . . . Bevo's *real!*"

"That whole book is waiting for me upstairs," he told her. "But it's in the dark, hidden away. I wish it could come the way the kits' stories come to me *dook-dook!* A flash of light, there they are!" He cut a giant piece of waffle with the side of his fork, ate it without losing his thought.

"Oi guff Urbon'f go'n to tak a lon tom." He reached for the milk, swallowed, noticed his wife's furrowed brow.

"I guess Urbain's going to take a long time," he repeated. "I'm not sure who he is, even, yet."

She nodded. "Classics must come slow. Anybody else would have given up on that book by now."

"Professional writer's an amateur who didn't quit," he reminded her. Then, for brighter conversation: "How's Novel Number Two?"

She smiled, sniffed the air. "It's coming along. Three thousand, sometimes five thousand words a day."

He laughed. "You're kidding. I mean really. How's it doing?"

"Really, Budge. Yesterday I wrote two chapters, fifty-two hundred words."

A sigh of understanding from her mate. "That's a long day writing."

She wrung one paw gently against another. "I wanted to slow down today, but Chantelle wants to run. I can feel it."

The sky turned high over the ferrets' little house, the wind sifting here and there, tamed by the porch so that it barely ruffled their fur, trembled their whiskers.

He decided to tell her. "I can't write kits' books anymore."

She looked up at him, surprised, frightened. "Oh? Why can't you write whatever you feel like writing?"

"They'll get in the way when it's time to publish *Where Ferrets Walk*."

She looked at him, puzzled. "Get in the way?"

"When my novel comes out, I want the world to take me seriously."

"Do you take Antonius seriously?"

"Danielle, he's an ancient, classical . . ."

"*The Ferret Fables.* Aren't those kits' stories?"

"I mean the modern reading public. Grown-ups. They'll think I write for kits. They won't read *Where Ferrets Walk* because Budgeron Ferret writes for kits."

Danielle smiled at her mate. "That's your fear speaking, isn't it? You know that's not true. It's not true for you, it's not true for anybody: 'I won't read his novel because he's written books for kits.' Readers love good books. What about Thartha? We'll read books by a *hedgehog* when she writes great stories!"

CHAPTER 17

A NIGHT OF DESPAIR, sleep like torn leaves, blowing, the scrape of claws on stone. *No matter how much I . . . this isn't working. It's never going to work.*

By dawn, not even the sun could lift his spirits. He would not survive unless he could be honest with his mate, he knew it.

So did she, setting breakfast upon the table.

"Something's wrong, Budge."

Silence for an answer, and a sigh.

"I'm not sure why I wanted to be a writer," he said at last. "Do I so love pain?" He nibbled a slice of mango, put it down. "Every day's the same. Do you want to know the truth? The novel is not coming. I'll never finish it. I don't love it, I don't even like it. It's empty. Disaster. A dragon showed up, he flamed me, Danielle, and he gnashed me to pulp. I'm a failure. I was lucky with *One Paw, Two Paws,* I was lucky with *Bevo the Hummingbird.* I'll never publish another book. We'll have to sell the ranch."

She crunched undismayed on almond-butter toast. "So who is this dragon, anyway?"

He blinked. "Hm? What do you mean, 'who is this?'"

"What's your dragon's name?"

The writer thought for a moment. Why, yes, it does have a name. "Cinnamon."

"What's Cinnamon look like?"

"Oh, come on, Danielle . . ."

"No, really, Budgie. If he's going to destroy you, at least you get to look at him, don't you?"

The writer closed his eyes, remembered. "He's bigger than the house, Danielle. He's blue, with wavy yellow stripes, he was painted from a merry-go-round. Teeth big green emeralds, sharp. Breathes flames, purple fire. Wings, but he doesn't fly."

"Your dragon won't fly?" she said, watching him over her toast. "Do you find that interesting?"

"You're sounding like a philosopher ferret, Danielle. No, he won't fly. And he doesn't want me to fly. Ever."

She looked at him wisely, nodded. "Does he have a title?"

"Title?"

"What's his job?"

"He's the Big . . . he's the Chief Really Bad Dragon."

"Can he hurt you?"

"He wants to. He wants to destroy me, he wants to stop me from writing, stop me from doing anything beautiful, ever again."

"Can he do it?"

Her mate was still for a moment. "Yes."

She set her toast gently on the table, leaned toward him. "How, Budgie?"

"He'll destroy me when I believe what he says."

"Are you frightened?"

"Yes."

"Let's see." Danielle leaned back. "Cinnamon's a flame-breathing Chief Really Bad Dragon three stories tall, scary colors, purple fire, but he can't destroy you unless you do the job yourself. To do that, you've got to believe . . . what do you have to believe?"

That instant, the dragon burst alive, scorched through her husband's terror: *"I'm a fraud, nobody cares what I think, my ideas are fake, my title's foolish, I'm foolish, I'll never write a book, I'll never change the world, I'll never do anything beautiful, I'm a failure, I'm worthless!"*

Budgie's eyes like spiral dinner plates, the echoes slashed cymbal razors through the ferrets' kitchen, deafening. The broken writer collapsed inside, fell back in his chair, eyes closed, tears of frustration beginning.

Danielle stunned into silence, the fur of her tail standing straight.

Then, slowly, as though she were one of those advanced souls who walk among ferrets, she took a deep breath, turned within, called her highest truth. When it answered, she held it fast.

She reached across the table, put her paw upon her mate's, spoke what she had been given to say.

"That's not you talking, Budgie, it's Cinnamon. Those aren't your fears, those are Cinnamon's fears! *Your dragon needs your help!*"

Budgeron opened his eyes, exhausted, unbelieving. "He wants to destroy me, Danielle. He wants to kill me!"

She listened to herself, scarcely believing it was her own voice. "Every image within us, every idea, comes to test our love," she heard herself say. "Even dragons. Cinnamon wants to be your friend, he wants to serve you, *he doesn't know how!*"

"He could start by not killing me. . . ."

Danielle blinked, reached to hold the blaze of inner light before it faded. "Give him a different job," she rushed on. "Not your destroyer. *Your bodyguard!* That dragon's your *muse!* Let him bring you ideas, let him light a ring of fire about you as you write, let him shield your characters from doubt, till they're finished at last and fly where you nor Cinnamon can ever go!"

Then the light was gone, a starburst vanished back to her center.

She was quiet for a long while, her husband staring at her.

She shrugged. "It's a thought. . . ."

CHAPTER 18

U PSTAIRS in his writing room, Budgeron Ferret closed his eyes, imagined a friend. Not my fear, he thought, I call forth my love, my most playful creativity . . .

"Cinnamon . . . "

No further than a whisper, there was a rustling in his mind, and a new Cinnamon, a thoughtful, devoted dragon, looked down upon the writer.

"What I wanted to tell you," said the great soft voice, "came from yourself. You already know. Urbain de Rothskit has something to say, but it's not for *Where Ferrets Walk*."

The writer listened. "Are you saying that I can't write historical novels?"

Ah, mortals, thought the dragon. They love to learn, they love to forget. "No," he said gently. "I'm saying you don't *want* to. You cannot write books that you do not love."

Budgeron pounded his paw on the table in frustration. "So what *can* I write, Cinnamon? You've hammered me flat, telling me what a failure I am!"

"I'm sorry," said the dragon. "I was afraid, it was the only way I knew to warn you, when I called you a failure. I meant, a failure you are with *Where Ferrets Walk*. Other books, you're a wonderful writer!"

"Thank you," said the writer. "I do have feelings."

"I'm sorry."

A long silence. "So what's my secret? No novel, no Rothskit? Now what? How do I write?"

"You've known it all along," said the creature. "The stories you wrote as a kit, *One Paw, Two Paws . . . , Bevo the Hummingbird*. What do they have in common?"

Anyone else, watching, would have seen a solitary ferret at the desk, unmoving, tranced in thought, computer screen humming blank before him.

Yet the author trembled with excitement, his heart raced in the midst of the test from this sudden new friend, his dragon muse.

"What do they have in common," Cinnamon prodded, "that your grand novel does not share?"

Instead of speaking, the writer's paws moved on the keyboard, he typed his answer:

I had fun, writing!

The muse waited, for the test was not complete.

I did not think about the writing, I stood aside, I got out of its way and let it happen.

A longer silence.

I was not critical of the writing while I wrote. It didn't matter what the reader thought, what the editor thought, it didn't matter what I thought. I let my story be what it wanted to be.

Budgeron heard a great sigh. "I don't edit," said the dragon, "but let's say you wanted to reduce those three to rules you might tape to your computer for now, or maybe for the rest of your life."

The writer clung to doubt, for safety. "Assuming I have a life."

The dragon smiled. "Assuming . . ."

Budgeron Ferret read what he had written. The fewest possible words. He cleared the screen.

Have fun, he wrote. Then:

Don't think. And:

Don't care.

"Ah!" breathed the dragon. "Simple. Fail-proof. True for any creative adventure."

The writer leaned forward, tense as a ski jumper launched down an icy chute. "Tape and scissors . . ."

"Not yet," said Cinnamon. "Test them. Test them on *Where Ferrets Walk.*"

Budgeron nodded impatiently, alone in his room. Of course.

"*Have fun?* No!" he said aloud. "That book was *work*. The opposite of fun, it terrorized me!

"Don't think? Ha! Mind squeezed flat, thinking. Instead of flying through the story I was *calculating*—should Rothskit do this, or this, or that? Should he do nothing? Maybe something else ought to happen now. . . ."

He nodded, agreeing with himself, beginning to understand.

"Don't care? Wrong. How I cared! Look out, world, here comes Budgeron Ferret! Hello, Medal of Avedoi Merek! What scarf shall I wear for the ceremony in Mustelania, when the Queen proclaims I've joined the greatest writers?"

It was true. How he had cared about that novel! How worried he had been, caring! Worried to a halt, a tin wood-ferret rusted under showers of stress.

"H'm." Cinnamon cleared his throat, interrupting. "See that? Each rule you followed, when you wrote your best. Each you broke, forcing *Where Ferrets Walk.*

"There's a time to work on a book and you know it," said the muse. "There's a time to think about the story, a time to care about your readers, your publisher, about rhythm and timing and grammar and spelling and punctuation, about design and advertising and publicity. But none of those times, Budgeron, is *when you're writing!"*

The dragon whispered, for underline, "None of those times is when you're writing."

Cinnamon craned his sea-blue neck, twisting to peer over the ferret's shoulder, to read the computer screen and quote correctly. "'Have fun. Don't think. Don't care.'"

"Thank you, Cinnamon."

"It's what I was trying to tell you. I had to get you away from Urbain de Rothskit. That book would have crushed—"

"Don't wreck it, don't wreck it, Cinnamon," cried the author in his mind. "Let me write!"

"Of course." With that, the giant lifted its head. In one movement, nearly a dance, he breathed a flaming circle about the writer, a wall leaping far above the animal's head. Yet from the flames came only a gentle warmth, as from a heart in love.

"You are proof from doubt, Budgeron Ferret," said his muse. "Have fun, and write."

All at once, listening, the writer was swept in a kaleidoscope of images, a colorswirl of possibility. Any character he could imagine was already enchanted. He felt a vast network of connections reaching out from him, drawing in.

Enchanted he was, by the wonder of his own mind.

Cinnamon towering, keeping the peace beyond that steep round fire, Budgeron Ferret was filled with hope and decision. Gone was the tension of quill and violet ink, the agony of which word to follow the last.

HAVE FUN! DON'T THINK! DON'T CARE!

Later he might come back to Count Urbain de Rothskit. Now, watching his paws move faster over the keyboard, he listened to his rules, and obeyed.

CHAPTER 19

H IS MANUSCRIPT was finished in a week, the same week that Danielle signed her contract for *Miss Mischief* with Ferret House Press.

After she brought a little snack for them to the porch that afternoon—watermelon sliced thin, currants on top—before she settled to her writing, he turned to her.

"Thank you, Danielle."

"You're welcome, Budgeron."

"What do you think?" he asked.

She smiled. "What do I think about what?"

"The new Bevo manuscript."

"A new Bevo? Where, Budge?"

He offered her a sheaf of pages, harvest of his pleasure, writing.

"Budgeron!" she cried, and read the title page. "*Bevo and the Bee Bandits*'!"

An hour later, Danielle was in tears. "How I love Bevo," she sniffed from her pawkerchief, "How I love *you,* Budgeron!"

He warmed in her praise, but listened to caution. "Are the bee bandits, at the start, are they too . . . well, too *mean,* keeping the flowers to themselves?"

"Well, they're not *ferrets,* Budgie! Those particular bees had room to grow, and Bevo did what no one else could . . . he showed them that flowers bloom for all the animals! I wouldn't change a word."

"It's first draft," he said.

"Perfect. I wouldn't change a word. I couldn't improve the story one bit. But you're the author." She smiled at him, a massive weight lifted. "You can change any word you want."

He took the manuscript from her, and the two animals sat together on the porch, the one drawing her typewriter near, continuing her second romance novel, the other . . .

The other licked the tip of his pen, began reading *Bee Bandits* from the top, listening to the sound of the story in his mind. Was the rhythm of the words as it must be?

Under his breath, he tested the meter, barely whispering.

"'Bevo hummed his way through the meadow, one flower to the next,'" he read, then the same syllables again, for the flow of them:

"Da-da *dah* da-dah da-da-da-dah, *da* da-dah da-da-dah . . ."

He liked the rise and fall of it. He changed nothing in the sentence, went down the page.

The second pass through his manuscript, he looked for the same word too often used. He smiled. Use a word once, the mind clings desperate, needs to use it again, right away. A writer sets boundaries: No.

Third pass, he cut every *just,* deleted each *very,* enjoying the way the sentences crisped and sharpened as they disappeared. It's all right to write those words first draft, he thought, it's not all right to print them later. With his pencil he worked a magic: the shorter the sentence, the more meaning it carries.

A mess of a sentence? he thought. Simple fix: don't print it. Cut it out. All the reader sees is what goes to press, final draft. It's not skill as a writer that matters, it's skill as a re-writer, over and again, each pass smoother, easier to read, till the final is a summer breeze over the harp of a reader's mind, soft telepathy. Open our eyes to these patterns of ink on paper, and in silence we hear voices, watch ferrets dance, fly with them on adventures we'd never imagine otherwise.

Fourth pass, he applied a different rule: the only synonym for *said* is *said,* and that one used sparingly. Don't use the word at all if you can get away with it. Show the character doing something, then follow with dialogue . . . you don't need *said*.

Once he had apologized to Danielle that his were little sto-ries for young ferrets, reminded her that his real destiny was *Where Ferrets Walk*. Yet in the quiet poet-garden of his heart, he loved his hummingbird. The tales that had come twice, now, divine flashes from some mystical nowhere, they thrilled him, brought him to laughter and to tears. He didn't know how to write any better than this.

So turned the summer afternoon, the two fluffy animals together, barely a paw's distance one from the other, each alert, unspeaking, trotting deep into vastly different worlds.

CHAPTER 20

"DEAR DANIELLE,

"I send this letter along with your first royalty statement to tell you that Veronique seems to be finding quite a few readers. There's word of mouth building for the book, and I'm happy to tell you that a week from Sunday, Miss Mischief will appear as number 13 on the Mustelid Weekly bestseller list.

"Congratulations from all of us at Ferret House!

"As we agreed, of course, we are expanding our advertising budget for the book.

"We respect your privacy, Danielle, but you've become a curiosity, and we've had quite a number of requests for interviews. Would you consider the matter again and think about talking with the press about *Miss Mischief*? Might you be available for television interviews, perhaps for a book tour as Veronique goes up the list? Let us know at your early convenience—it could matter to sales.

"I must say, Danielle, that we can't wait to see your second novel. Of course we wouldn't want you to feel any pressure, but if we had a manuscript in our paws soon, a story as arresting as *Miss Mischief,* it would be possible to place it in our fall catalog and in bookstores by the holidays.

"We remain,

"Your friends and obedient servants,

"Beatrix Chateauroux Ferret, Vice President, Publicity Director"

The check that accompanied the letter was a quiet underline to her publisher's enthusiasm.

Like any first-time author, Danielle had been delighted simply to see her book in print. She hadn't considered what might happen if it were to become a bestseller.

Now she sat back in her writing chair, tapped the envelope softly at the side of her nose. If publishers measure success by numbers of copies sold, she thought, how do authors measure it—by the chaos it brings into their lives?

She was happy with their choice to move to Colorado, happy to stay with Budgeron on their ranch. What would he do if she went off on some many-city tour for her bestseller? Quality of life, she thought, is more important than book sales.

Danielle set the check aside. Then she stood, took the letter to the kitchen, tore it into small pieces and scattered them in the wastebasket. Bestseller or not, she wanted to stay at home.

CHAPTER 21

No SOONER had she fluffed the batter and ladled the first batch into the waffle iron than she heard a sound on the stairs. Budgeron Ferret appeared in the kitchen doorway, a sheet of paper in his paws.

"Done!" he cried. "I've finished my novel!"

She looked at him dumbfounded. "Finished, Budge? Did you say finished?"

"You heard it. I am done with *Where Ferrets Walk*!"

She took the page from him, scanned that old first paragraph and read the remainder:

The dawn he watched was the beginning of his own new being.

No more the burdens of aristocracy for this Rothskit, he thought. The theater has called, and I shall answer!

With that he packed a single valise, left a note declaiming that he would rather live a full life as a thespian than a troubled one as a Count, and set off across the horizon for the city, in search of his star.

The End

Danielle looked up from the page. "Budgie?"

Her husband studied her, eyes alight, a great weight gone from his shoulders.

"This," she asked, "is *Where Ferrets Walk*?"

"I didn't want to leave it unfinished."

"Budgie?"

"It's a short literary novel. I realized, upstairs, that I don't write classics. It's a bestseller title, but I don't know how to write the book. It wasn't fun for me. Too heavy. Couldn't run."

"Don't throw this away," she said, handing the sheet to him. "I have a feeling . . ."

He touched the page in her paw. "No. It was everything I could do to keep from shredding it, upstairs."

"Budge . . ."

"Don't worry, Danielle. Sometimes the way to save a story is to throw it away. If it matters, it'll come back again, different clothes."

Not long after, as he installed a telephone extension under the kitchen cabinet, the phone rang at the instant Budgeron connected two wires, the sudden noise jerking him away as though he had touched raw voltage.

He answered on the third ring, while his wits returned.

"Why, Vauxhall! How good to hear your voice!" It was quiet as Budgeron listened to his publisher, to the one who had believed in him and in Bevo, who had fast become his friend.

"Not for us. Colorado summer: if you don't like the weather, wait five minutes, it'll change. . . ."

Danielle came to sit on a tall stool by the sunny kitchen island, listening to her mate's side of the conversation.

Why the call? she wondered. Something nice is going to happen, I know it.

"Yes, sir. You could move your office from Manhattan to Side-Hop. There's a whole block empty by the feed store, you could rent it cheap."

A long silence. "You do? Vauxhall, thank you!"

She looked at him, raised her eyebrows, held her paws in front of her, more information, please. *What's he saying?*

"I'm so happy to hear that! I can't tell you how good it feels, that you would . . ."

This is no social call, she thought.

"That's a pretty big audience."

He turned to Danielle, made a wide face to say he couldn't believe what he was hearing. "Wow!" he whispered to her.

No matter that he couldn't believe it. She could. There's no competition in writing, she thought. The only place Ferret House Press can get a Budgeron Ferret book, from now till the end of time, is from Budgeron Ferret. Anything else is imitation.

"*Every* writer wants a publisher who's committed to the books. . . ."

Vauxhall, she thought, wants another Bevo story. He would not have called unless the Bevo books were selling very well indeed.

"Of course I will. I'll give it careful thought."

Danielle furrowed her brow, whiskers forward, thoughtful.

"I will. And hers to you, Vauxhall. Thanks for calling. Bye."

She waited. Then: "What did he say?"

Her husband looked at her in disbelief. "Vauxhall sends his warm regards."

"Yes. . . . *Tell me!*"

"He likes *Bevo and the Bee Bandits*."

Danielle jumped from the stool and hugged her mate. "Of course he does! Hurray, Budgie!"

"He wants me to write Bevo books. It's not just the kits who like the stories, he says it's parents, too. Grown-ups. They're buying Bevo for gifts, now, and once that happens, he said there's no stopping."

"Did you tell him you don't want to get typecast, a kits' writer?"

"No."

"Why not?"

"You taught me better. Ferret House wants a contract for more books. Three more."

"A *three-book* contract?" At once she curbed her delight, watched him closely. "What do you think about that?"

"For so long I thought the novel was my destiny. Did I come here to write *Where Ferrets Walk,* then *not* to write it?"

"You were put on this planet to do your highest best," she said. "If it were your destiny to write Urbain de Rothskit, you'd write him and nothing in the world would be big enough or strong enough to keep you from it."

"*Where Ferrets Walk* was not my book, Danielle. I don't write literary novels!"

She heard beneath his words. No distress, no self-pity, Budgeron was no martyr speaking. A fundamental change had happened within him, before her eyes.

She smiled at him. "'Listen to your life,'" she quoted from *Bee Bandits,* "'it's telling you all you need to know about the creature you can become.'"

He listened, stretched luxuriously against the kitchen island, feeling more relaxed than he had been in a long time. "I think my life's telling me to stay away from quill pens and exotic ink for a bit. Forever, I think. The creature I want to be, right now, is the one who writes the adventures of Bevo the Hummingbird."

CHAPTER 22

AT NOON, two days later, Danielle Ferret heard a sound from the living room, a cry, a scream from her mate shattering the gentle noise of her typewriter.

"*Budgie!*" In a flash she was up, her chair flying midair away from the writing table, she a sable blur into the house.

She found him frozen at the television set, his fur standing straight, his tail bottlebrushed, one paw both reaching and repelling the screen. "Danielle . . ."

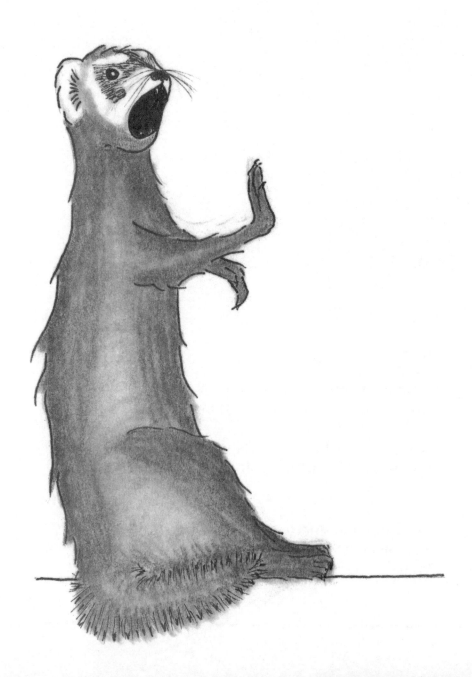

Her eyes followed his paw; she gasped:

Where Ferrets Walk

The title dissolved to a book-lined study, a slow zoom to a close-up of a distinguished host in soft hat and satin ascot, turning a giant globe with one paw.

"Good afternoon. I'm Brytham Ferret. Welcome to *Where Ferrets Walk*."

The two animals watched, openmouthed.

"Our program this week takes us to the coldest spot on earth, where one risks one's life even to visit . . ."

The study faded, the narrator continuing, his voice carrying over a scene of ice and snow blown horizontal by a great wind. ". . . where Lola Evine Ferret has set up her camp. She is under siege, night and day, by the wind and the cold. It is a siege that she is determined to survive."

From the snow, the face of a sturdy ferret appeared, layered in heavy scarf and parka hood, frost clinging to her mask, to eyelashes and whiskers.

The narrator spoke directly into the scene. "It looks a little chilly, Lola!"

The adventurer laughed over the storm. "Why, no, Brytham, this is one of our warmer days. . . ."

Danielle touched a button and the screen faded to black.

She turned to her husband, her face a veil of shock.

"*Where Ferrets Walk*? Budgeron, how could they . . ."

He fell into his soft old chair. "A great title, but not for me." He laughed, free as a song. "I write for kits!"

There was silence for a little while, both animals watching the dark screen, reflecting on coincidence.

"Nothing just happens, does it, Danielle?" he said at last. "How long did it take for me to get the message? Urbain de Rothskit never took off, not at all. My dragon roaring

Don't write that book, it's going nowhere! He says my characters will live forever: I think Rothskit, he means Bevo. No sooner do I let the big novel go, my publisher calls, he doesn't want a big novel, he wants a Bevo series. I turn on the television, *Where Ferrets Walk* is nobody's book, it's a TV show!"

She smiled at him. "What's the difference between dedicated and stubborn?"

"Why, Danielle," he replied, "dedicated, we're in tune with our life. Stubborn, we're not!"

CHAPTER 23

Next spring, they were in print, pyramids of them in bookstore windows: *Bevo Makes a Promise. Bevo in the Haunted House. Bevo Takes a Nap.*

All that Budgeron Ferret had hoped for *Where Ferrets Walk* came true for Bevo the Hummingbird, each new title more popular than the one before. *Bevo Takes a Nap* was hailed on the lofty pages of *Mustelid Weekly*: "The most absorbing volume on the nature of imagination this reviewer has read—words for kits, meanings for ferrets everywhere."

Danielle delivered her second novel to Ferret House that summer. As shocking as *Miss Mischief,* the exotic Chantelle-Dijon Ferret ravaged a swath through three continents, wider than naughty Veronique's. Chantelle's startling white mask and her secret quests for the good of ferrets everywhere earned *Forbidden Questions* an opening spot at number 4 on the *MW* bestseller list, just below the author's first book.

They were on the way from Side-Hop to Florence for delphin treats, humming around the curve south of the city, they saw it at the same instant.

"Budgeron!"

At once their little truck pulled off the road and rolled to a stop, dwarfed under a billboard the size of a jumbo jet:

Mustelids read

Danielle Ferret

Kits read Bevo

at bookstores everywhere

The two sat transfixed, the sign towering over them. Then, out of the silence, her voice:

"What have we done?"

Until that moment the ranch at Side-Hop might as well have been a glass dome over the writers, sealing them away from the shock waves, the one gentle and the other scandalous, that their books were causing among readers.

Manuscripts had been reams of paper from Side-Hop Office Supply, stories that they read to each other, puzzling, smoothing, polishing, correcting over and again till they disappeared in the mails.

Stories changed into contracts and royalty checks. In time, each of them accepted that their books were bestsellers. They were happy for this, but writers do not turn through the day in amazement that their books are appreciated. All the excitement distant to them, news reports from far-off places.

The billboard towering above, however, was no report. It stood 80 paws high, 150 wide, the letters three times taller than Budgeron himself, carbon ink against sun white. Ferret House had increased its advertising budget as promised.

"If this is happening in Colorado . . ." he said.

". . . What have we done?" she murmured.

In time the truck moved on, the driver and his mate silent. When they loaded oats and grains and fresh apples from the yard at Manny Ferret's Delphin Treats, the clerk at the feed table looked at their invoice, looked again.

"You'd be no relation to *the* Budgeron Ferret, now, would you be?"

MUSTELIDS READ

DANIE

"Do you have mangoes?" Danielle asked at once. "My little Dusty loves dried mangoes."

"We certainly do, ma'am. In fact, they're right in front of you, on the counter."

They retreated west to Side-Hop, reaching the quiet of the ranch by nightfall.

The two ferrets, they loved telling stories. The gifts they offered were the worlds of their imagination: the saucy lands of Danielle's heroines, the enchanted territory of Bevo's innocent adventures. When we give sparingly, ferrets are taught, sparingly are we rewarded. When we give worlds, we are rewarded vastly.

They had prepared for what they could plan and control: hours at the computer and the typewriter, writing to deadlines, discussions long-distance with editors and book designers and subrights salesferrets at their international desks.

Yet neither had given more than a passing thought to what they could not control: the storms of curiosity their books would sweep down upon them, the forests of choice, the fields of surprise ahead.

From that moment under the towering letters, their lives would never be the same.

CHAPTER 24

"Whoa, Lucky," said Budgeron, shifting his weight in the saddle. "Whoa down."

The chestnut delphin slowed to a stop, Danielle halting alongside on Dusty.

Sunup found the two at the far edge of their property, out of sight from their ranch house in the savannas to the north. Wicker saddles creaked softly beneath the riders, cool air fragrant with prairie grass and cottonwood about them. The murmur of the Little Side-Hop River bent in a wide curve nearby, a few paws deep over patches of watercress and smooth round stones.

"Vauxhall's leaving it up to us, a book tour. Good for sales, he said, but I'm not sure I want to go, Danielle. The city was all I knew till I got away to Monty's that summer, and then city again after that. Now I'm happy here. I don't want to go back to cities."

She laid her reins lightly on Dusty's mane. "I love it here, too."

"We don't need to go on tour. We don't need to sell books. They're already selling."

She nodded.

"We have everything we want in Side-Hop."

The barest breeze began, early sun warming the hillside. Here and again, the silent flap and flash of butterflies.

"What do you think?" he asked. "What should we do?"

"I don't know *should*."

He smiled, leaned forward in the saddle, massaged Lucky's neck. "What do you want to do?"

"I'd like to go."

"Why?"

"To see how it feels," she said. "I think, out there, we may be celebrities. I don't know what that feels like. I'd love to meet our readers."

"Cities?"

"It won't be for long. I don't mind cities. That used to be home." She reached across the space between them, touched his faded old ranchpaw bandana. "A tour sounds like fun, doesn't it? A vacation, a little break from writing? We'll learn a lot. And if we don't, that's the end of it."

"Remember the billboard? We'll be mobbed."

She smiled at the image. "Ferrets don't mob, Budgie. If readers come to say hello, I'd be happy to meet them. Wouldn't you?"

He smiled, shyly. "I am a little curious . . ." Then: "Danielle . . ."

She looked at him.

"This is going to be your tour. You know that, don't you?"

"It's going to be our tour," she said. "Both of ours."

He shifted his weight forward; Lucky started a walk, heading for home. "It will be you and me, yes, but there's a difference between a kit's bestseller and an adult's bestseller. Vauxhall told us straight: it's *Miss Mischief,* it's Veronique that's got everyone startled. I'm going to stay in the background and watch. You know that's the way I like it, a little attention goes a long way with me. I'll have my moments with the kits, but you're going to be the one out front."

Danielle nodded, but inside she who had read to kits knew the truth: her books wouldn't be in ferrets' libraries a century from now, Budgeron's would be.

CHAPTER 25

THE TWO WRITERS left Side-Hop for Manhattan one sun-blue morning on a sleek polished business jet, courtesy of media magnate Stilton Ferret, distant relative and close friend of Vauxhall.

The captain met them as they boarded, a powerful animal dressed in pilot's cap, sunglasses, a scarf of deepsky blue and four golden stripes. As the writers reached the top of the airstair steps, the officer removed his glasses:

"Howdy, ranchpaws."

Budgeron was tumbled in a wave of delight, a voice from his past. He knew that smile.

"Strobe!" he cried. "I can't believe . . . *Strobe!"*

The friends embraced, time collapsing around them: the flash of Monty's vast ranch, their whistles and cries over the thunder of Rainbows on a run, the clang of old-West dinner bells.

The captain stood back and looked at the writer. "Comin' up in the world, are you, Budge?"

"Well, I'll be." Budgeron turned to his wife. "Danielle, here he is! This is Strobe, from my ranchkit days!"

The flier took her paw, touched it gently to his nose. "My pleasure to meet you, ma'am."

His friend was taller, leaner than Budgie remembered; he wore the air of command as easily as his captain's scarf.

"You can step this way, if you'd like," he said.

The jet sparkled, full-length couches of finest Rainbow wool, soft chairs, dining tables of polished wood, the corporate logo inlaid golden letters: *MusTelCo.*

"The president's lounge has the best view," said the captain. "Long way from a saddle on a sheep drive, though I suspect you may have guessed that." He winked at his friend, went forward to the flight deck, leaving his passengers in the care of a flight steward and two attendants.

After takeoff the captain invited the writers to the cockpit. Danielle, drowsy already from the whisper of sky by her window, elected to nap on the president's couch.

Budgeron went forward to the seat tactfully vacated by the copilot and donned the officer's headset. Flight and engine instruments spread before him, through the broad windshield a view of the world as he had never seen it, Strobe sitting relaxed at the controls to his left.

They cruised in bright sunlight at an altitude of thirty-seven kilopaws, Earth unrolling below as the two stitched in the seasons since they were ranchkits.

Once Strobe held up his paw to Budgeron, pressed the microphone button on his control wheel. "Minneapolis Center," he said, "MusTel Two Zero, level at three seven zero." Then he turned once more to the friend he had known since before he had learned to ride.

"Things moved on. Seemed like no sooner home from Monty Ferret's Rainbow Sheep Resort and Ranchpaw Training Center," he said, "than it was time to drop out of college and meet some airplanes."

"You quit school?"

The flier nodded. "One semester in academia, Budge, that was enough for me. I told my folks they could save the money. I wanted Action . . ."

Budgie joined him, a line the ranchkits had shouted so often: ". . . Adventure! Romance on the High Plains!"

They laughed together.

"I found it all, flying, Budge. Student pilot, mail flier, crop seeder, flight instructor, charter pilot, freight dog, airlines . . . a lot of flying."

Strobe lapsed into quiet, remembering, then continued, "I didn't know my roommate from school was going to become quite the media mogul. Stilton found me again, asked me if I'd look over his airplanes, make some suggestions. I did. After a while, he asked me to be his chief pilot." The captain smiled. "Sure beats sloggin' through mountains at night, Budge, covered in ice, dodgin' treetops, wishin' you were somewhere else, preferably warm and On The Ground."

"I'm proud of you, Strobe," said Budgeron. Cathode-ray tubes showed airways in green lines, compass heading in white, airports passing below in blue. His friend had mastered all of this.

"Proud of you, too. May angel ferrets help me if I ever need to survive, putting words on paper!"

The writer learned, cruising just under the speed of sound, that their ranchkit pal Boa had joined the Ferret Rescue Service, stationed on the storm coast of Washington State.

"What he could do with tools!" said Budgeron. "Remember that old tractor, back of the delphin barn?"

"Rusted shut," said the pilot. "Even Monty said, 'Not much hope, kit, that machine's gone.' Remember?"

"Boa had to show us."

"Good old Boa," the captain said. "I'd like to see him again, before too much longer."

"Alla?"

"Last I heard, Alla was digging up ancient cities."

"She did it! She's an archaeologist!"

The captain nodded. "She called once, a while ago, through New York on her way to Persia. We had dinner, she couldn't talk enough . . . 'We've found the lost city of Pheretima!' That's some vast big palace under the sand, I guess. Cut out of the rocks. Our little ranchkit figured out where it was buried. 'Facts behind the legends! Where did we come from?' You know Alla. She gets her mind set. . . ."

Over Cleveland, the pilot gave Budgeron a flight lesson, gentle turns, small climbs and descents. "You learn flying in five minutes," he said, "you spend the rest of your life practicing."

The writer practiced, easing the jet left and right, surprised at how swiftly it answered his touch. "I'd show you some extras," the pilot said, "but there's this bell goes off down in the Air Traffic Control Center. We go three hundred paws off our altitude, they get all excited, call and ask us what's wrong. It's more fun, on a nice day, flying the biplane down low than it is the jet up high. Maybe we could do that sometime."

"I'd like that. Don't forget." Budgeron took his paws from the controls, gave the airplane back to the captain. "Are you married, Strobe?"

His friend smiled. "Odd you should ask. Not long ago, I would've told you it wouldn't happen. Last month I met Stormy. She was flying south over the Siskiyous, through some ferocious weather, flying a cargo plane, warned me about it on the radio. I was flying north, warned her about the storm I'd just come through south. Turned out we both landed at Redding, had dinner together, we've called each other since. She's a good kit, a good pilot." He paused. "I'm crazy about her, Budge."

Starting their descent into Manhattan, the copilot returned. Budgeron gave up his seat and stepped back into the luxury behind the flight deck.

Landed, engines shut down at the terminal, the captain swung out of his seat, smiled to them. "I guess I can tell you now. I'm scared of heights and scared of crowds. When that door opens, you two are on your own!"

Danielle hugged him warmly. "Thank you, Strobe. It couldn't have been better, you showing up for Budgie today."

"It was him showed up for me, ma'am."

The flight steward touched Strobe's shoulder. "Exit door's clear to open, sir."

"If you two survive what's about to happen," said the pilot, "I'll see you for the flight to Boston. Good luck, old friend!"

Strobe gripped Budgeron's paw again, touched his cap to Danielle, then pressed a button by the entrance and the door slid upward.

A sea of fur surrounded the arrival gate, fur in colors of snow through polished coal, a crowd of dark-mask faces, light masks, faces maskless, paws waving. *Welcome Danielle Ferret!* painted on signs. *Welcome Budgeron!* Kits in hummingbird hats, *Bevo Loves Me* embroidered.

Danielle swallowed, looked at her mate. "I didn't expect . . . ," she called over the noise of the crowd.

He patted her, reassuring. "This is fun."

She touched above her ears, self-conscious. "Is my hat on straight?"

Black velvet, soft and shiny, a bill of polished brass angled so low it nearly hid her eyes. He touched her fur lightly. "You're beautiful."

She led the way, smiles and waves for the first crowd of fans she had ever met.

Now Budgeron followed Danielle and watched, proud of his mate. As they love her saucy heroines, he thought, so they love the author who brought them to life.

A moment before they plunged into the crowd, a young animal appeared, held up her paw.

"I'm Beatrix Chateauroux," she said over the noise, "Ferret House Press. We've got a table set up . . . cameras . . ."

They touched noses, left and right, and the publicist led the way through the crowd. No one pawed the authors, no one pushed or shoved. A path opened ahead of them from the crowd's respect and courtesy.

Beatrix touched a switch on the microphone. "Welcome, everybody!" she said. *"Welcome Danielle and Budgeron Ferret!"*

The cheers and waves redoubled, signs in many colors, tilting left and right:

We Love You Danielle Though We're Not So Sure About Veronique!

Call Me . . . Valka!

Here Comes Veronique!

Two kits atop their parents' shoulders, holding a banner: *Hurray for Bevo!!*

"On behalf . . . ," said Beatrix. Cheers. "On behalf . . ."

The cheers continued, and finally the publicist passed the microphone to Danielle.

"Thank you, Manhattan," she said. "It's wonderful to be here!"

Budgeron Ferret didn't know whether he was watching a marvelous transformation or discovering what had been there all along. Danielle, the volunteer reader to city kits, the pawdicurist friend to each of her clients, the writer who invented naughty ferrets turned nearly as noble as the readers for whom she wrote, was an angel in the cameras.

"Why, she's a star!" He nearly turned to see who had spoken when he realized they were his own words. His mate was as born to celebrity as queens are born to rule.

"If Veronique were here," Danielle said quietly, letting the microphone amplify her calm, "she'd be planning a way to steal the spotlights. But it's just Budgeron and me, and we're so glad that you came to say hello."

The cameras loved her. Her brushed fur reflected television floodlights in rippling silver sheens, it sparkled bronze and gold in the swish of flashbulbs. Her image in the monitors, from the jaunty angle of her cap to the tip of her ebony tail, was chiseled elegance.

Danielle wasn't acting, she was enjoying every animal in the crowd, and everyone knew it.

Budgeron looked into the faces of her fans, imagined they were mirrors of the one onstage in front of them. They wanted her to be charming, to be spicy and unexpected, they wanted her to reflect their own inner selves, and they were not disappointed. The love between writer and readers, as she spoke, was a warm aura that filled the room with light.

He felt a tug at his knee, looked down to see a kit standing by her father, her mask still faint as dust. She clutched a stuffed hummingbird half her size, and Budgeron knelt to her level, below the sea of fur.

"Thank you for Bevo," she said softly, thoughtful of the crowd listening to Danielle, watching Budgeron with solemn dark eyes.

"You're welcome!" The writer patted her Bevo doll. "I'm happy he's your friend."

"They weren't bad bees." The dark round eyes held his own. "They're my friends, too."

The room blurred for Budgeron Ferret. He hugged the kit and rose, touched her father thanks, brushed his eyes with a paw. This is what writing's about, he thought. You hold an image within, you love the sight of it, and you hand it to a reader. Images, ideas, characters, dialogue, all these things come like torches, to warm and to light and to pass from one of us to another.

"She loves *Bee Bandits*," her father said. "We just got *Bevo Takes a Nap*. Her grandmother read it, she called this morning, told me stop whatever I was doing, go down now, today, and buy this book for Kimra! Then we saw in the paper that you were going to be here."

"Thank you," said Budgie, "thanks for coming."

"Would you mind?" The father opened a bag, produced the book and a pen.

Budgeron steadied the book on his knee, wrote, *Kimra! The bees are your friends always,* and signed his name. Then he sketched a kit and a hummingbird and a bee, flying together toward a cloud.

He closed the book and returned it with the pen to the father.

There was a burst of applause as Danielle finished her talk. Chateauroux took the microphone, told the crowd that Danielle and Budgeron would be happy to sign books for a while, then they had to be off for television interviews downtown.

So went the first hour of their book tour.

CHAPTER 26

Piet and Olga Ferret owned Black Mask Books, in the heart of the city. Now they watched as patiently as their customers, curious to find what kind of animals these writers might be.

Their business was books, their love was books, as well. The touch of a fine cover, the delight of a thoughtful phrase or a funny one in ink and paper, the lift of a beautiful story, the sparkle in a reader's eye: "It's just what I was looking for!"—these made their lives and their work a glad place.

"Welcome to Black Mask!" said Olga. Would they notice, she thought, the hours we spent painting banners, would the writers see the posters and advertising, their books stacked floor to ceiling, three tries getting them all to balance?

"Thank you," said Budgeron. "We . . ."

"Beautiful!" said Danielle, embracing her, touching noses. "How much time you've taken for us! And the little bees circling . . ."

Piet looked at his mate and relaxed. Business would be good, but more important today, customers would meet the souls behind the bestsellers, would know that books are not mystery, they come from the hearts of ferrets as easy to meet and talk with as these two. They were one family, writers and booksellers, it warmed them both to meet.

Readers stood in line, talking with each other, making friends as they waited, most of the way around the block. Over the door a taut banner:

Mustelids read

Danielle Ferret

Kits read Bevo

Surprising owners and readers alike, Danielle trotted down the line, touching noses here and there with her readers, told them thanks for coming, then bounded inside to the table at which she would sign their books.

"That's different," said Olga, watching.

"Nice touch," her mate replied.

Unlike the publishers who had rejected the manuscript of Danielle's first book, Olga and Piet knew it for a bestseller at once, ordered a hundred copies from the Ferret House rep. Within days, they had followed with an order for three hundred more.

"Veronique's so *naughty*!" her readers told Danielle over and again while she wrote their names and signed her own. "If my mother knew I was reading *Miss Mischief . . .*"

"If my mother knew I was *writing* it," said Danielle, and they'd laugh together, two conspirators, author and reader.

The more she met them in person, the more Danielle loved and respected the ones who read her book. Most of all, she learned, they're playful. They know their highest sense of right and they live by it, every one of them decent loving animals. Yet every one of them eager to pretend that within there roams an impudent, a defiant, a brazen ferret, shocking friends and family with every free-spirit leap and bounce.

Meeting readers was a telepathic burst of understanding, each of them to the other, and they laughed without words in the minute they shared together. Contact energy crackled through the moment; it would take hours, later, for the writer to settle down.

"I write for fun," she told her readers. Yet it was more than fun that they found in her books, she thought, and as she signed she reached for the answer. It was an *unleashing* that happened, when certain animals opened her pages and entered her world.

Her husband had told her long ago that she didn't need to please everyone with her stories—if a book pleases only half of one percent of the reading public, though no one else bought a single copy, it will be a massive bestseller.

"It's not that you're different from me, Danielle, that I like your books," one reader told her while she signed *Forbidden Questions,* "it's that you're the same!"

Budgeron's place might as well have been a different world. Hers was a square desk, a solid square sign with her name and photograph. His was round, a cloud of feather hummingbirds suspended from threads, turning in the air.

No lines of ferrets standing patiently for his signature but clumps of kits, sometimes brushed and orderly, sometimes animal-wrestling, mouths wide, little fangs bared, tails bottlebrushed and flailing before their minute with the writer.

Many brought crayoned pictures of Bevo, presents to the author. Suddenly poised and polite as their turn came to have books signed, the littlest of them turned shy for that moment, too bashful to touch noses with Bevo's creator.

He signed and sketched in their books, hoping his Bevo-drawing and words for them might be valued later on.

What would this have been, he thought, if instead of Bevo this book were *Where Ferrets Walk*? There'd be no kits here, no unruly thumping about, but everyone grown-up, solemn and literary. Deadly dull.

The television show's choosing its title was the best thing that could have happened to his troublesome novel. He smiled to himself as he signed. Whatever will become of Count Urban de Rothskit?

The next kit was barely tall enough to see over the edge of his table, the only sign of her a snowy chin on the wooden edge, a dusty mask and tiny whiskers, two black eyes, a little voice:

"Will you write *Bevo Meets the Count* for me?"

The writer caught his breath, thunderstruck. "Excuse me? *What did you say?*"

The eyes did not blink. "Write *Bevo Meets the Count,* please."

The writer stared speechless at the kit, turned open-mouthed to her mother, unbelieving.

The parent shrugged. "It's just an idea."

"Where did she . . . how did she . . . ?" said Budgeron, a shock of confusion. "Did she say *Bevo Meets the Count*?"

"She's having trouble with numbers."

"Numbers?" He leaned forward, hoping to understand.

"She wanted me to ask you to write *Bevo Learns to Count* and I told her she could ask you herself."

Budgeron Ferret began to laugh. He stood, lifted the kit to the table, where she looked up puzzled and solemn to her mother. What had she done? Kits waiting, and their parents, smiled at the sight.

"Forgive me," said Budgeron to the kit's mother. "I thought she said . . . What she said, it's brilliant, it's a stroke of unbelievable . . ."

He threw up his paws, helpless before coincidence.

He took his seat again, asked her name, then wrote: *Seraja! Thank you for saving my life! From Urbain de Rothskit and . . . Budgeron Ferret.*

Still smiling, he handed the book down to her and she took it, huge in her little paws.

"Thank you, Budgeron Ferret," she said.

"You're welcome." You have no idea what you've done, Seraja, he thought. *That's* what his destiny wants for Urbain de Rothskit! *He meets Bevo the Hummingbird!*

And yet, as he watched them depart, the kit and her mother turned and winked to him in exactly the same instant, then raised their paws together, a synchronized wave good-bye before they set off again and disappeared from sight.

A shock of strange went through the writer, one shock, then another.

What was that? What happened? Was it coincidence, I didn't hear what she said, or did I hear that little voice perfectly well? Did those two come to have a book signed or were . . . or were they angel ferrets disguised, or philosopher ferrets, come to hand me a story I would never have found without them?

He watched the place where they had disappeared, the open doorway to the street, sidewalk crowds passing by. Ferrets don't wink like that, he thought, not a mother and her kit together, knowing the depths of another's heart.

Of course, *Bevo Meets the Count*! he thought. Brilliant brilliant brilliant! The *contrast* between the two, one the very spirit of light, the other heavy and lost. When they meet! What will the Count discover? Will he find something more profound in the little hummingbird than all of Europe's aristocracy?

Whoever you are, the writer thought, turning back to his table, mortals or discarnates or wise and thoughtful creatures . . . thank you!

When the next kit held her book up to be signed, the writer watched her closely. "What do you know," he asked the little face, "about angel ferrets?"

CHAPTER 27

THEIR HOTEL SUITE was not far from Ferret House Press. Convenient and expensive, thought Budgeron. Sixty floors above Madison Avenue, the corner window looked out across the city, north to the park, west to the river and beyond. Beyond was Colorado.

He missed his home. He missed the morning air, he missed the hills and the river, he missed Slim and Lucky and Dusty. He remembered when he had loved the city for its excitement and drive; now those qualities made him yearn for the slow side of life, the peace of Side-Hop, the solitude of the ranch.

From their suite's center table burst a massive spray of flowers, a curving rainbow turned still life over a bottle of sparkling snow-water and a card from the publisher: *For Danielle Ferret—Miss Success.* The card was a miniature bestseller list, *Miss Mischief* circled in scarlet.

On a side table stood a wicker basket of small chocolates, lifted nearly airborne by cherry-color balloons. Painted on the basket: *For Bevo—The World's Favorite Hummingbird!*

Budgeron turned from the window, walked into the next room, sighed and collapsed into the deep satin hammock.

"What do you think?" he said. "How's it going?"

She appeared in the doorway, looking tired. "It's hard. It's fun. I miss home."

"We'll be home before we know it. Only seventeen more cities."

Fatigue faded to determination. "I'm glad we came. I like my readers."

"Me, too. Mine are different from yours."

She brightened. "What happened? I looked over and you were . . . startled. Something happened."

Budgie told her about the strange incident, the coincidence, twice he misunderstood what the kit had said.

Danielle shrugged. "Philosopher ferrets."

"Maybe. And what would they say? 'Forget the coincidence, *write the story!*'" Budgie looked to the ceiling, an ornate white-on-blue fresco of classic Greek ferrets. "What would Urbain de Rothskit do if he met Bevo? He'd simplify! And if he simplified, what would he find in all the world that mattered most to him?"

The two of them talked till late on the grand satin hammock.

Before they slept, Danielle turned to her mate. "Are we successful writers, Budgie, you and me?"

He thought about it. "Do we love our books?"

CHAPTER 28

H E WOKE while the city slept, unable to silence the little voice: "Will you write *Bevo Meets the Count* for me?"

No computer, no typewriter, he slipped silently from Danielle's side, found his pen and note cards. He padded softly to the living room of the suite, touched the lamp switch, curled in the corner of the sofa.

It was all there, the story, barely a whisper from Cinnamon. Simple, breathtaking, inevitable. He watched it happen, he wrote what he saw:

Away in the sky, a speeding sunlight dot above the snowy clouds of Hungary, flew a tiny lime-ruby streak. Bevo the Hummingbird was off to find Count Urbain de Rothskit, the actor ferret who had awed and charmed a continent.

The tiny bird could not imagine why, but as he rolled and dived through the mist toward Rothskit's castle, he knew that the Count was frightened. . . .

CHAPTER 29

Hours later, after the interview for *Celebrity Ferrets* and before an afternoon of satellite television appearances, Danielle and Budgeron met with Vauxhall and the staff of Ferret House Press in the executive conference room.

It was a catered lunch: palettes of bright fruits, swirls of walnut butter, flakes of chocolate, Colorado mountain snow-water while the animals talked.

Until they saw them in one room, the writers hadn't known how many ferrets worked together to bring their books to the marketplace. The art director was there, Tricie, a little shy around the powerhouse her designs had helped to create. Danielle's editor, Marla, of course, met for the first time in the fur. Erich from Production, Angella from Copyediting, Paul from Subrights, Bonbon from Advertising, Mirabelle, Chateauroux's assistant, from Publicity . . . animals funny and thoughtful, eager and retiring, ferrets who, like the owners of the Black Mask, lived under the magic of the printed word.

A giant paw covered her own. "Markham Ferret, Inks On Paper. I want to thank you for a lot of business lately! Wouldn't miss the chance to meet you, Miss Danielle, if I had to stop the press!" He grinned. "Of course I didn't have to do that . . ."

Vauxhall had invited librarians as well, friends of years, stories to tell.

"*One Paw, Two Paws,* Budgeron, our collection went to five copies, then ten, checked out all the time! Katherine looked at me one day, your book returned one minute, it went out the next, she told me, 'Darryl, it's going to happen to this kit! We'll do well to keep an eye on Budgeron Ferret!'"

Librarians cherish collections, booksellers count sales, Budgie thought. What matters for both is ideas to readers.

For everyone in the room, writers were not merely interesting ferrets, they were essential to life. Without writers, none of them would be here . . . the kindness to the visitors was beyond courtesy, it was as kindness to parents, every bit genuine.

In a while all took their places at the table and Chateauroux joined the meeting, handing a sheaf of papers to the company president, finding a chair across the table from the writers.

"Are you two holding up all right?" she asked. "Paws tired from the autographing?"

"Stronger and stronger," said Budgeron, flexing his paw. It was true because he said it was. Had they admitted fatigue, the two would have been exhausted.

The publicist smiled. "You like the meetings, face-to-face?"

He nodded. "My readers are guests in my mind while I write. I like them there, but they're awfully quiet."

"They tell me I'm not alone," said Danielle. "I may have an odd sense of humor, but so do they."

Chateauroux nodded. "I stood in line yesterday, talked with a lot of your readers. They're not going to go out to become the Veronique of Fifty-seventh Street, but they're awfully fond of her, they like her pepper. They're fond of you, too, Danielle."

Budgie sensed something in the air. He listened to Chateauroux, but he watched Vauxhall studying the papers she had set before him.

The president looked up, glanced at the tall old clock in the corner, pendulum swinging as it had for decades. Talk around the table went still.

"You have a busy schedule, you two. Satellite interviews, then *City at Night,* then you're off to Boston?"

"We've confirmed, Vauxhall," said Chateauroux. "Half an hour on *Round the World* from Boston, before the *Sunrise* show."

The president nodded, smoothed his whiskers. "Budgeron, Danielle," he said. "Ferret House has been in business a long time. Some of us have worked here quite a while. And we've found something that happens over and again. You probably know this, but it's why we're together right now. An idea gathers to itself everyone it needs in order to be born."

The ferrets of the staff nodded to themselves. It was true.

"The idea of Bevo found Budgeron to write him. Veronique found Danielle. Then after a while Bevo and Veronique found all of us at Ferret House. Now they're flying to readers around the world. An exciting business, publishing; it never gets old."

Vauxhall leaned toward the two. Silver fur gleamed in his mask, his face the picture of the thoughtful, distinguished book-ferret. "From everyone at Ferret House, we're happy you're here. I expect that you two will be getting all the attention you can stand, and maybe a little more. Frankly, we can't print your books fast enough. *Bevo*'s as successful a book as kits' publishing has seen, *Miss Mischief*'s is in her fourth printing . . ."

Chateauroux held up a paw close to her body, claws spread wide.

". . . in her fifth printing," said the president. "I know you've got a lot on your minds just now, but I want you to know that we'll do whatever we can to keep you happy with Ferret House for a long time."

There was a ripple of applause from the animals who had worked so hard to turn the writers' ideas from manuscript into copies in every bookstore. They didn't envy them, they didn't want to be Danielle or Budgeron, but glad they were to know that their own work and skills had launched the authors' books into the world, made it a more exciting place for readers.

Budgeron turned to watch his mate. Fur brushed, eyes bright under the bill of a crimson cap, her mask sharp and clear, she sat poised and lovely.

"Thank you, Vauxhall," she said, "thank you all. You believed in Budgeron from the beginning, you brought me aboard when no one else wanted Veronique. We won't forget."

Chateauroux had taken a call on her cell phone, now she nodded to the president.

"Your limousine awaits," he said, and rose. So did everyone else in the room. "Thank you, Danielle, thank you, Budgeron, for taking time with us all this morning. I trust you'll enjoy what's about to happen to you. You have a quiet place, there in Colorado?"

They nodded.

"Maybe you'll want a bit more land around you if you can." It was a congratulation and a warning. "Before too long that's going to mean a lot, a quiet place to write." Vauxhall extended his paw to Budgie, then to Danielle. "Have a good tour."

In the limousine, Chateauroux handed Danielle the latest copy of the tour schedule, along with a large white envelope, then turned to the driver.

"To the studio, please, Gabby.

"There's just one small change in the afternoon," Chateauroux said to the writers. "We're swapping the satellite interview for the Houston station with the one for Wichita. Not to worry. We'll have a card up, under the camera, with the city and the interviewer's name. Oh, and I almost forgot. We had a call from Cheyenne-Montana Productions. Are the film rights for *Miss Mischief* available?"

Danielle looked to Budgeron, startled.

He told her what she already knew: "That's Jasmine Ferret." He grinned at his mate. "It's about time she called."

CHAPTER 30

NOW THE WHITE envelope from Ferret House lay open on the deep silk hammock in the penthouse suite of the Boston Princess Hotel.

"I've never heard of so much money in my life!" said Danielle for the third time since they'd read the offer from Ferret House. "Budgeron, do they want to pay me this . . . this fortune, just to run off and have a good time writing?"

Her mate lay back into the luxury of a giant satin hammock. "No, dear, they want to pay you this fortune for three finished manuscripts. Of course they'd like you to have a good time writing, but it's those stories that Ferret House wants in its paws. The sooner the better, a bonus for sooner."

She stepped into the hammock, rested her head near his, went suddenly silent. At last she sighed. "Shall I do it? We don't need the money. . . ."

"It isn't about money, Danielle. It's about your writing, it's about your characters, your spirit, about what you mean to readers. You give who you are, the money follows. What you do with the money, there's a different test."

"The publicity, the crowds," she said, bringing his fears out for another look. "Do you want to be a celebrity, Budgeron?"

"Do we decide? We're famous if other animals say we are. We can't control what they think. Somebody's never heard of us: 'So who's Danielle? Who's Budgeron Ferret?' Celebrity's not up to us, it's up to them."

"We could stop writing. . . ."

He stared at her.

"Well, we could," she said.

"I'd like to see you try."

She laughed. "Could you?"

"Of course I could. Soon as I finish *Bevo Meets the Count*. After that, I'm out of ideas."

He nodded, happy for his mate and for the adventures ahead. We chose this life, he thought, we asked for it, and now it's showed up on our doorstep.

CHAPTER 31

Her characters visited Danielle Ferret day and night, chatty spirits unable to end the séance with their author.

Awake in the dark, Budgeron listened to the sound of her pen on the notepad, a small sliding hiss in the dark, ink on paper, words she would puzzle over in daylight, glad for her notebook, deciphering tilted night-words into scenes that would have disappeared by dawn.

He breathed in silence, not to disturb her.

Not that she needs notes, he thought. Danielle Ferret never starved for ideas. More than any other animal he had met, his mate knew the ferret condition, the turns and mysteries of ferret relationships. And as she knew, she wrote.

The sound stopped, the sleek head sank into her pillow. Then she lifted her head barely clear of the pillow and turned to her mate. "I love you," she murmured in the dark, the next second back to sleep.

He was stunned in warmth. Incredible that she would say that, not a tenth awake!

What have I done, he thought, that I deserve this beautiful creature to love me?

Budgeron Ferret sighed happily, reached a paw to soothe the animal beside him. She relaxed at his touch, turned toward him in sleep. In a moment her breathing was deep and even once more.

Writing, he thought. What a blessing to have been given the talent; what a test, learning to use it.

Then he slept.

It was an ancient city, in his dream, buildings of granite, streets of cobblestone around the town square. And yet the rooftops . . . he knew those rooftops.

Budgeron Ferret, an audience of one, listened to the town crier, a black sable ferret in red cap and golden scarf, reading aloud from a wide parchment scroll:

"'You have found what every writer has found before, what every writer who follows must find as well.'"

The crier looked at him for a moment over the scroll, his eyes meeting Budgeron's. "And this, too, will you find . . ."

He spoke as if he were reading, but his eyes held Budgeron's: "The more ideas you have, the more shall you be given!"

Behind the crier, Budgie saw the roofs of those houses again, the top of one so deeply familiar. . . .

"You enchant an inner family of characters who will come if you invite, each bringing stories for you to set in words."

There was a long silence, waiting.

"Do you invite?"

"Me?" he replied in his dream. "Do I invite? Invite who? Ideas? Characters?"

The same question, firmly asked: *"Do you invite? Yea or nay?"*

He was not accustomed to his dreams demanding answers. "Yea, I invite!"

The crier looked at him, nodded, those black eyes watching his own. "So let it be."

Then the ferret rolled the scroll firmly, tied it with a dusky ribbon. Whatever ceremony there had been was over.

"So let it be," he said once again to Budgeron, the voice warm and informal. Then he was gone.

The writer turned in the dark, sleepy, puzzled. A message dream. What was the message? What did it mean?

CHAPTER 32

THE WIND eased along the meadow beside the Little Side-Hop River, grass and cattails swaying in the last hour of day, hill shadows stretching eastward toward the dark.

"It's beautiful here, Budgeron."

He nodded.

"Look down the meadow," she said. "If we galloped fast enough, do you think we could fly? Up from the grass, into the sunset, out over the housetops of all the cities . . ."

The words struck him like thunder. Over the housetops. The housetops . . .

The image from sleep came rushing back, the town crier, the housetop of his dream. Of course! It was his own roof he had seen, the top of his kithood home!

He closed his eyes tightly, reaching for the image from sleep. Why? Because, he thought, because . . .

"Budge?" Danielle called, gentle, not to interfere. "Where are you?"

"Dandelion!" he cried. *"Buttercup!"*

At once they crowded round, set loose by remembering. In the attic, he thought, they're still there! All his friends, all the animal dolls his mother had sewn and stuffed for him.

Danielle touched the reins, Dusty trotted close.

"Growing up, Danielle," he said, aflood in memory, "it wasn't just Bevo! There were dozens Mom made for me! Dandelion and Buttercup were baby giraffes, sisters, yellow-flower pajamas. Did I tell you?"

He looked at her, his mind full of bright times back then. "I'd pick an animal from the shelf, we'd sleep and dream together, adventures every night!"

His mate smiled, seeing the pajamas.

"Once I picked the sisters," he told her. "Dandelion said, 'Let's imagine we're going to Africa.' Not Buttercup: 'I'm scared of Africa. It's full of wild animals. I don't want to go.'"

He grinned, remembering, telling the story. "'*You're a giraffe!*' said Dandelion. 'You *are* a wild animal! You *came* from Africa!'

"Buttercup stared at her sister, Danielle. 'In my *jammies?*'"

Danielle laughed at the picture, for the joy that Budgeron had found in the sunlight of his memory.

"And there was my bat, my amazing bat, Bvuhlgahri. He took me to Mustelania, to the palace." Budgeron slipped into the brooding, low voice of the kithood creature: "'Your Majesties, may I introduce Boucheron-Bvuhlova . . .'"

His eyes were bright in the sunset, remembering. "The stories, Danielle, the stories!"

"Your mother. How many animals did she . . . ?"

"Twenty! More! Aviator Bear, White Buffalo, my dragon . . ."

"Dragon? What color dragon?"

"Blue, wavy yellow stripes . . ."

"Oh . . ."

"Seahorse, Hedgehog, Dinosaur, Orca Whale, Blue Whale, Raccoon, Zebra . . ."

"Where did you . . . ?"

"Every night. We'd travel the world, Danielle, everywhere. Petey, three feathers left, my peacock from Hawaii . . ."

"Budgie Ferret's friends," she said quietly. "Where are they now?"

"They're in the attic, right now. All of them. They're in the attic, back home. . . ."

No sooner in from the stable, he raced to the telephone, lifted the receiver, dialed.

"Hi, Mom!"

Into Side-Hop airport, Express Mail, arrived boxes 1 of 4 through 4 of 4. In each box, old friends: yarn smiles and bright shoe-button eyes through faded colors and careful patches stitched. Petey the bird in box 1, Dandelion and Buttercup traveling together in box 3, Zebie and Camie with them.

For anxious moments Budgeron thought his bat had been lost. Then at the bottom of box 4: *"Bvuhlgahri!"*

The black had faded to gray, but there he was, same soft wings and fluffy face, same high radar-squeak when the ferret squeezed his velvet body.

The writer was a kit once more. "Bvuhlgahri, can we fly again? Do you remember?"

In his dream, the writer had invited his friends to return, and return they had, into his waking life.

Before sunset their shelf was fixed in place, same as it had been long ago, within reach of a paw from the hammock. The old stories could be dreamed anew.

Budgie Ferret's Friends, the books were called.

The first manuscript of the series went directly to Vauxhall Ferret.

The day it arrived, the president and chief executive officer of Ferret House Press canceled his appointments, closed the door to his office high above Madison Avenue.

There being no cover letter, Vauxhall began as would any other reader, at the title page.

The pages flowed through his paws, exotic blossoms in warm honey.

Budgie's passage to Africa, holding tight the manes of twin giraffes, the night on the veldt when all the creatures told their stories, the scene at the Great Waterfall where they parted, at the entrance to The Undiscovered Place. His discovery of the secret that wild animals keep for ferrets everywhere. The test of the Gift, and Budgeron's return, giraffes once again become fluffy dolls upon his bedroom shelf. His Final Question, and proof of every ferret's Wild Powers.

Vauxhall read the book through, then turned to page one and read it again, slowly.

When he had read the last page once more, he put the manuscript down and looked out his window.

It means so much, he thought, to live a life that makes a difference. How can an animal do that? How can a writer touch a keyboard far away, without a sound, reach me here in the city and remind me who I am? Books, he thought. Books.

CHAPTER 33

ONCE IN A WHILE, in the silence under Western star-fields, Budgeron Ferret was brushed by the life that might have been, had ever he finished his giant novel.

Now and again random images flickered from sleep: the author of *Where Ferrets Walk* the keynote speaker at writers' conventions, Budgeron Ferret in formal ascot, the Avedoi Medal for Literature gleaming at his throat.

A different future, he sighed, missing that different past.

Then in the dark, for the first time, he realized, that's no life that might have been! I couldn't write that book, I couldn't force that life to happen! I still can't, he thought, I don't want to.

I don't like literary novels!

He eased from the hammock, not to disturb Danielle, and padded to his writing room. Today, he thought, I am open to whirlwinds, adventures with any character, any inner friend who needs my paws to tell a story. I am open to write what I enjoy.

On his desk from the day before, two letters, reader mail. Curious, he lifted the first.

It was printed with the Mustelanian coat of arms, beneath it in small sharp letters: *The Palace.*

"Dear Budgeron Ferret,

"In the short while since we were chosen from the Librarians and elected King and Queen of Mustelania, we have had many tests, many decisions to make about our past and future and our highest right.

"Not long ago we realized that the principles we've needed in our decisions are the ones you wrote so simply in *One Paw, Two Paws, Three Paws, Four Paws.* Your book is a focus of the highest ferret wisdom—what we loved as kits we practice today to lead the kingdom.

"Thank you for our education."

It was signed in sweeping letters: *Prestwick & Francesca Ferret.*

The second letter was neatly printed by a pencil evidently held in a very small paw.

"Dear Budgeron,

"I love Bevo the Hummingbird.

"Sometimes when I need to know the right thing to do, I ask Bevo in my mind.

"But before he tells me I already know and he likes that a lot."

It was signed in careful, slow cursive: *Bosco Ferret.*

The writer held both letters for a long moment. He had not written the Great Ferret Novel. He was not invited to writers' conferences or to literary teas. His opinion was not sought by the press.

He lived, however, with a loving, brilliant mate on a hilltop ranch deep in a gentle countryside. He shared his mind and skills with his muse, a large and thoughtful dragon.

Budgeron Ferret had chosen to be a writer. With his choice came poverty, loneliness, rejection, frustration, despair, perseverance, delight, attention, riches, love, understanding, fulfillment, a life of ideas that mattered to him, shared now and then with kings and kits.

Without thought, without care, words on paper for the fun of it, he closed his eyes and wrote what he saw:

The land where we touched was green as spring meadows, the mountain a color of summer maple, the fields below sheets of clover, the lake broad and deep as autumn. Atop the mountain, a palace of golden snow.

Upon the fields lay a village, thatch-roofed, misty smoke curling from chimneys as ferrets stirred awake.

I turned to Bvuhlgahri Bat, flown so far to bring me here.

"Mustelania," came the low, dark voice. "And in the farthest, deepest depths of Loch Stoat, Boucheron-Bvuhlova, for a thousand years, a great serpent has waited."

"Waited . . . ?"

Rushing on, paws blurring over his keyboard, the writer wondered: Is a serpent like a dragon? What color dragon?

"A thousand years, the serpent has waited," he said. "For you."

And so it happened, as rosy-whiskered dawn pushed her nose under the tent of night, that Budgeron Ferret's writing room dissolved, Mustelania coming alive about him.

He watched and wrote. What would happen next?

Ferret House Press